Dangerous Attra...

Dirk couldn't believe he'd let Joni get that close to danger. He should have foreseen it or done more to prevent it.

Something had changed between them last night. Joni had plugged into a long-buried need, connecting him to her and, in an inexplicable way, to himself. The prospect of harm coming to her was intolerable.

Heck, how much more of an explanation did he require? She was the mother of his child, essential to Jeff's happiness. If for no other reason, Dirk would have gladly laid down his life to preserve hers.

"I'm staying tonight," Dirk said. "I'll sleep on the sofa bed."

Long lashes curtained Joni's eyes as she considered. She faced him across the den. "You don't have to stay on the sofa."

His body responded instantly, viscerally. After last night, he knew how warm her mouth would be and how quickly she would come to heat.

But he didn't dare let down his guard again.

ABOUT THE AUTHOR

Jacqueline Diamond spent a year after college traveling and writing in Europe. Since then, she's been a news reporter, a TV columnist, the author of more than twenty Harlequin romances and, above all, a wife and mother.

Books by Jacqueline Diamond

His Secret Son
Jacqueline Diamond

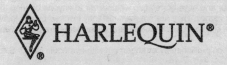

TORONTO • NEW YORK • LONDON
AMSTERDAM • PARIS • SYDNEY • HAMBURG
STOCKHOLM • ATHENS • TOKYO • MILAN • MADRID
PRAGUE • WARSAW • BUDAPEST • AUCKLAND

ISBN 0-373-22512-1

HIS SECRET SON

This edition published by arrangement with Harlequin Books S.A.

® and TM are trademarks of the publisher. Trademarks indicated with
® are registered in the United States Patent and Trademark Office, the
Canadian Trade Marks Office and in other countries.

Printed in U.S.A.

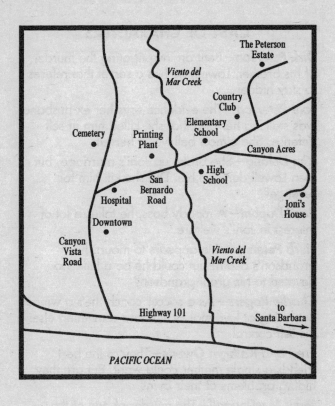

The Peterson
Estate

*Viento del
Mar Creek*

Country
Club

Elementary
School

Cemetery

Printing
Plant

Canyon Acres

San
Bernardo
Road

High
School

Hospital

Joni's
House

Downtown

Canyon
Vista
Road

*Viento del
Mar Creek*

Highway 101

to
Santa Barbara

PACIFIC OCEAN

CAST OF CHARACTERS

Dirk Peterson—Bent on investigating the murder of his brother, Lowell, he has a secret that refuses to stay hidden.

Joni Peterson—The evidence says her ex-husband was stalking her and that she killed him in self-defense. She almost believes it herself.

Kim Delong—She broke up Joni's marriage, but then Lowell dumped her. Did she kill him for revenge?

Basil Dupont—A moody boss, he takes a lot of interest in Joni's welfare.

Herb Peterson—He appears to mourn his grandson's death, but could he be a little too devoted to his great-grandson?

Charlie Rogers—As a soccer coach, he's a winner. But losing at love makes him lose something else: his self-control.

Fred and Kathryn Owens—They're the best friends a single mother could want. But are they hiding problems of their own?

Terry MacDougall—The murder of one of the town's leading citizens makes him eager for a quick arrest, and all the evidence points to Joni.

Celia Lu—The lonely lady next door turns up at the most inconvenient moments. Maybe that isn't entirely by chance.

Chapter One

Joni Peterson was removing her TV dinner from the microwave oven when the phone rang. Reaching for the plastic container with pot holders, she let the answering machine pick up.

"Hi, it's Joni! If you're calling me or Jeff, please leave a message!"

She wasn't surprised when the caller hung up.

Through the kitchen window, she could see the twilight fading across her patio and small backyard. A crisp October breeze ruffled her roses and the brush on the hill beyond.

Near the edge of the dense woods above the house, a neighbor's gray-striped cat prowled, then vanished into a shadow. Seconds ticked by, but there was no further sign of it.

When she bought the house last year, Joni had relished the privacy. Now the remoteness of the place made her uneasy.

A few drops of steaming sauce from the fettuccine Alfredo plopped onto the back of her hand as she set the plate on the table. Instinctively, Joni lifted the burned spot to her mouth to take away the sting.

Maybe she should have grabbed the phone. It might

have been her eight-year-old son, Jeff, calling from his friend Bobby's house half a mile away to tell her he'd forgotten something for his sleepover.

But if it had been Jeff, he would have left a message, she told herself firmly. Besides, he spent the night at Bobby's so often that he kept an extra toothbrush and sleep shirt there, so what could he need?

She scooted into her chair and picked up the newspaper to read while she ate. As usual, she'd barely had time to glance at it in the morning before leaving for her job as public relations assistant at Viento del Mar Community Hospital.

The phone rang again. Joni picked it up. "Hello?"

A click, followed by a dial tone. Darn him! The man knew exactly how to irritate her. Although she'd signed up for Caller ID, the man had his number blocked.

So far, he'd been careful. The calls hadn't been frequent enough to spark any action by the phone company. The other harassment—roses cut from her bushes and left on the porch to wither, a pair of sunglasses taken from her unlocked car and set on her patio—wasn't threatening enough to concern the police, an officer had told Joni when she called.

No one was going to arrest Lowell Peterson for anything less than a major crime. As the owner of Peterson Printing, one of the largest companies in the central California town of Viento del Mar, her ex-husband wielded a lot of power.

As she rinsed the plastic tray and tossed it in the recycle container, Joni kept expecting the phone to ring again. Where was he calling from anyway? His home? His car?

The shadows deepened on the hill behind her house.

On the patio, a breeze rattled the loose pedal on Jeff's

bike. She made a mental note to tighten it and to remind him to put his bike in the garage. Maybe she should put it away now, but there was no rain in the forecast. A night outside wouldn't hurt it.

Joni retreated to the den, their combination guest room and electronic haven. Kneeling by the video rack, she picked out an old favorite, *The Sound of Music.*

As she stood up, she found herself face-to-face with a group of photos on the wall. The largest, taken three years ago, was a formal portrait of her, Lowell and Jeff. She'd hung it there in an attempt to keep her son's life as normal as possible.

The photographer had posed them on risers so that the gap in heights wouldn't be so apparent. Even so, Lowell had a commanding presence. Tall and blond, with a piercing light blue gaze, he'd swept Joni off her feet when she was a nineteen-year-old clerk and he was the son of the company's owner. Five years her senior, he'd already been pushing for a dynamic expansion of Peterson Printing.

Studying his photograph, she could feel the excitement of being singled out by him. Her amazement at discovering the intensity of his interest had enabled her to hold her head high on their early dates, even though she knew she didn't fit in with his country-club friends.

Joni wasn't sure what he'd seen in her. She'd been described as interesting-looking, with her high cheekbones and slightly crooked nose, but never beautiful. Certainly it hadn't been her rather boyish figure that attracted him.

How much had she really loved Lowell, and how much had she been awed by him? It was a bit late, Joni told herself ruefully, to worry about that.

Slipping the video into the VCR, she sat back to enjoy

Julie Andrews and the Rodgers and Hammerstein songs. Half an hour later, she realized to her relief that the phone hadn't rung again. Maybe Lowell had better things to do tonight than make a pest of himself.

She was immersed in the movie when the wind picked up loudly enough to be heard over the TV. Storm coming, she thought absently. The forecasters had been wrong, as usual.

A crash from outside set her heart racing. The metallic jangle reverberated down to her bones.

The bike! It must have blown over. "Oh, for goodness' sake," Joni grumbled aloud. The last thing she felt like doing was going out into the nippy air and hauling Jeff's bike to the garage. Yet if a storm really was starting, the patio's cover wouldn't offer much protection.

Joni turned off the VCR. In the service hall by the back door, she pulled on an old sweater and stuffed her feet into a pair of canvas slip-ons. As she let herself out, she flicked on the patio light. Its glow penetrated no more than a few feet into the gloom.

"Here, bikey, bikey." The wind tore away her feeble attempt at humor. Moist and chill, it blasted through the sweater as if it were a cobweb.

She should have remembered to bring a flashlight, she thought, but going back inside was silly. She wanted to get this chore finished as quickly as possible.

In the faint light, the patio chairs stretched grotesquely. Unable to distinguish between shapes and shadows, Joni banged her thigh against the glass table. She let out a couple of swearwords she would have suppressed had Jeff been home.

Wind gusted against her back, bringing the first drops of rain. Strands of shoulder-length hair whipped free of her bun and scrambled around Joni's face as if attempting to flee.

By the time the breeze quieted, her eyes were adjusting to the dark. She could make out spoked tires and twisted handlebars lying on the concrete a few steps away.

Another blast of wind hit, and something arced through the air. As Joni dodged, she recognized the object as the hummingbird feeder she'd filled this morning.

The glass globe had been a Christmas present last year from Lowell's grandfather, Herb, who doted on Jeff and remained Joni's friend. It was a beautiful feeder, but if she hadn't moved so quickly, the darn thing would have beaned her.

Near the garage, a shoe crunched on concrete. The hairs on her neck stood on end.

"Who is it?" Beyond the patio, she couldn't see a thing.

"It's me."

She recognized the tenor voice and the footsteps coming toward her, firm and confident, with an occasional scuffing noise as if he were impatient to be moving faster.

A tall shape loomed into the porch light. She stared in dismay at her ex-husband.

No wonder he hadn't made any more phone calls. He'd come to confront her in person.

"Joni, are you all right?" A frown creased the face worthy of a men's magazine. Strong, symmetrical, rugged.

Lowell wore a designer suit and an open-collared silk shirt. What the well-dressed man wears to stalk his ex-wife, she thought furiously.

"What are you doing here?" Rain misted her face and

the wind tugged more hair from its knot. On the hillside, bushes swished.

"It's not what you think." He stopped a dozen feet away.

"What is it I supposedly think?"

"That I've been harassing you."

"So here you are, sneaking around my patio after dark," she retorted. "Obviously, this disproves the whole idea."

"Where's Jeff?" he asked abruptly.

Joni's alarm deepened. Why did he want to know? Was he planning to attack her? If he thought their son was home, he might not risk it. "Asleep," she said.

"No, he's not. I saw you come home alone."

He'd been watching her. Goose bumps crept along her skin. "Lowell, please leave," she said. "Jeff's at Bobby's house. They'll be bringing him home any minute."

He eased forward. The hunter, not wanting to startle his prey. One large hand reached toward her arm.

"Joni, surely you don't believe I would—"

A blast of chill air ripped away the rest of his words and a thrashing noise from the slope made Joni turn sharply. As she did, something bashed into the side of her head with a crunch.

The world spun madly and her mind filled with pain beyond enduring. She barely felt her ribs hit the spokes of the bike as she fell.

Chapter Two

Joni's head ached and her side throbbed. The patio was a jumble of dim light and confusing, lumpy shapes.

She wondered if this was a dream. Then she became aware that she was soaked and profoundly chilled.

She ought to go inside. She had to move.

Her numb hands flexed with difficulty. In her right palm, she discovered, lay something slender but hard. When she gripped it, it felt like the haft of a kitchen knife.

"Hello? Are you here, Joni?" The voice with a Chinese accent belonged to her neighbor, Celia Lu. From the sound, she was walking up the rise from her yard.

Joni tried to answer. All that came out was a grunt.

A flashlight beam swept through the mist. "Hello, anyone?" Celia called. "Who is here?"

This time, Joni managed to prop herself up enough to catch the light in her eyes. Pain sliced into her head and she fell back.

"You are hurt?" Celia hesitated at the edge of the patio. A childless woman in her fifties, she had moved next door about six months ago. Lonely during her husband's absences on business, she came over frequently to chat. "I call for help?"

Joni hated to involve the police or paramedics. In view of Lowell's prominence, the incident would be sure to make the newspaper. But she couldn't handle this alone. "Yes, please," she whispered.

"Someone else is here? I hear noises. A shout."

"Lowell. I guess he's gone." But why would he leave her here, injured?

Celia played the flashlight across the patio. It wavered and stopped on a dark shape. Her mouth opened and out came a high-pitched needle of sound that went on and on.

The scream merged with the throb in Joni's head, pulsing at the same frequency. Consciousness shattered into a thousand shards, and silence returned.

WHEN JONI AWOKE, two men wearing light blue jackets knelt beside her, one holding an umbrella while the other checked her pulse. Brightness turned the patio a violent white against a rippling silver curtain of rain.

Her clothing was soaked with a sticky substance that Joni recognized as hummingbird nectar. Her head must have smashed open the feeder.

To her right, she glimpsed figures bending over something. There were three people: a uniformed officer, a man in a plaid sport coat who scribbled on a pad, and a woman taking photographs.

"What happened?" she muttered, and caught a startled look from the paramedics.

"Detective!" one of them called. "She's awake!"

The man in the plaid coat continued making notes. "Yeah, yeah, I'll be right there."

When he moved, Joni saw a crumpled shape on the ground beyond. A portable floodlight picked out disarrayed blond hair and the expensive weave of a gray suit jacket marred by a dark stain.

"Lowell?" she asked.

The detective skirted some broken glass and crouched beside her. "Mrs. Peterson? I'm Detective Terry MacDougall."

All she could murmur was "Lowell—is he all right?"

"I'm afraid he's dead," the man in the plaid coat said.

Joni didn't hear whatever he said next. A rushing noise filled her brain, a combination of dizziness and disbelief.

Lowell? Dead?

Their divorce two years ago had been bitter, following Joni's discovery that he was having an affair. That had been the last straw after years of his sarcasm and domination.

And yet he could be warm and funny, especially with Jeff. Lowell had been a towering figure in her life. She couldn't accept that he was gone forever.

Right after she left him, he'd harassed her a few times with phone calls and petty vandalism. That had soon stopped, though. After Joni asked for only reasonable child support and agreed to generous visitation rights, Lowell had even apologized.

A few months ago at his request, they'd begun having dinner together occasionally to discuss Jeff and reestablish a friendly relationship. It had lasted until a few weeks back—when the harassment resumed. Lowell denied being behind it, but the actions were exactly the sort of thing he'd pulled right after they separated. Joni just wished she knew why he'd started in again.

Now he was dead, and she might never know. Even though she'd felt anger and resentment, she'd never wished Lowell any harm.

His death would hurt people she cared about—Jeff and his great-grandfather, Herb. It was going to affect a lot of other people, too, in ways she couldn't even begin to think about.

The police detective was kneeling next to her, waiting with a look of strained patience, and she caught him glancing at her right hand.

Hadn't she been holding a knife? It was gone now; maybe she'd dreamed it.

"You...found—"

"We're keeping the knife as evidence, Mrs. Peterson," the policeman said. "Would you care to make a statement?"

"I didn't kill him," she said, and saw in his face that he didn't believe her.

Lowell must have been stabbed, she thought. But he was so strong. Who could have done this?

The detective asked her to describe what had happened. After she did, he asked her the same questions again, as if trying to trip her up.

She didn't understand why he seemed so accusing. It *was* odd, awakening with a knife in her hand, but even if somehow she'd wielded it, she would only have done so in self-defense.

What did the man think she had to gain by murdering Lowell? As he excused himself to confer with the photographer, his voice gave her a clue. He used that pseudorespectful, subtly mocking tone that some people adopted when addressing the rich.

He thought she'd done it for the money.

Lowell's wealth, including the ownership of Peterson Printing, would presumably go to Jeff. And therefore, until he grew up, to Joni. She didn't want it, but she doubted the detective would believe her. On TV, people killed for money all the time. Maybe some did in real life, too. But not her.

The police would be even more suspicious if they learned that Jeff wasn't Lowell's biological child, but she hoped the medical records would remain confidential. Besides, to Joni, the boy *had* been Lowell's son.

She just wished she could remember exactly what had happened tonight. If she could explain how she came to be holding the knife, maybe she could convince the detective of her innocence. But her mind remained a blank. As she'd told MacDougall, she recalled exchanging a few words with Lowell, and then nothing.

Finally, the policeman gave the paramedics the okay to remove her. They fitted Joni with a cervical collar to protect her head and neck, then gently lifted her onto a gurney.

As they rolled her to the ambulance, she saw Celia standing on the sidelines, staring at her with mingled horror and fascination. It gave her the bewildering sense of being some stranger in a newscast instead of her ordinary self.

The doors closed and the ambulance jolted forward, sirens screaming. Joni's mind began to fade.

At the hospital, she slipped in and out of consciousness most of that night and early Thursday morning. She felt the needle pricking her hand to start the intravenous tube. She heard the diagnosis: a concussion and bruised ribs. She listened to carts rattling by in the hospital corridor and voices on a distant intercom, but still she remembered nothing of what happened to Lowell.

The nurses seemed solicitous, bringing extra pillows and laying a cool cloth across her forehead. Joni's public relations duties included interviewing staff members for the in-house newsletter. Apparently, she'd generated some goodwill, or perhaps, as she hoped, they were this kind to all the patients.

Later that morning, she finally came awake. The first thing she did was to call Bobby's mother, Kathryn Owens.

"I'm so sorry," Kathryn said earnestly. "I heard on the radio what happened. But the boys don't know."

"If you or Fred wouldn't mind driving Jeff to Herb's…"

Joni hated to impose. Over the past few years, the Owenses had done her more than their share of favors. But her son needed someone close to give him the awful news about his father, and the best person was his great-grandfather.

"Of course we don't mind. Jeff knows the address, doesn't he? And we'll stop by your house and pick up some clean clothes for you." Her friend knew where Joni hid a key. "You'll need something to wear when you leave the hospital."

Joni started to thank her, but Kathryn waved it away. "I know you'd do the same for me."

"Of course," she said. "But I hope you never need it." Thank goodness for friends, Joni thought as she hung up. Without them, a single mother could scarcely survive.

Around noon, she heard raised voices in the hall and recognized the gravelly tones of her boss, Basil Dupont. The nurse was refusing to let him in until the doctor gave the okay for visitors. He in turn refused to leave a potted plant until he could deliver it in person. For a public relations director, Basil had a remarkably dour personality.

Finally, he went away, taking the plant with him. She dozed again, awakening when the nurse came in with the clean clothes Kathryn had dropped off. The woman also carried a large flower arrangement in a vase. "A man brought this while you were asleep," she said, and handed Joni the card.

"Get well soon," read a masculine scrawl, followed by a signature. Charlie Rogers, her son's soccer coach. That was sweet, Joni thought.

The last time she attended a practice, he'd come over afterward to talk and seemed on the verge of asking her out when the Owens family stopped by. He'd been kind to come and visit her, Joni thought, but, all the same, she was glad she hadn't had to make small talk.

By late afternoon, her mind cleared enough for her to sit up and read the newspaper. On the front page was a photograph of her and Lowell that had been taken five years ago at a charity concert. In happier times.

Rain pelted against the hospital window. The dark mood suited Joni as she studied the reporter's words, trying to let reality sink in.

Printing company owner and country-club board member, Lowell Peterson, was found fatally stabbed on the patio of his ex-wife, whom he was suspected of harassing. The police have declined to release information about the murder weapon, but unconfirmed reports say a kitchen knife was missing from the cutlery block on the kitchen counter.

Although rain has destroyed much of the evidence, police say it appeared that the former Mrs. Peterson confronted her husband and an altercation ensued. Mrs. Peterson sustained a concussion and bruised ribs.

The cuts on Mr. Peterson's hands and arms are

believed to indicate his attempts to fight off the knife attack...

All the pieces fitted. Except that Joni hadn't taken a knife when she went out to the patio.

It was possible, however, that she had left it on the glass table a few nights ago while barbecuing. She couldn't be sure she'd brought the knife inside.

Could she have killed Lowell and not remember it? Joni didn't want to believe it, but especially after suffering a head injury, she couldn't completely disregard the possibility.

The newspaper ran a lengthy biography of Lowell. His honors during high school. The student offices he'd held at nearby University of California, Santa Barbara. His prominence in the community.

Joni stared at her former husband's chiseled features in the photograph. Once upon a time, he'd swept her into the clouds. Unfortunately, she'd had years to sink back to earth under the weight of his critical, controlling behavior.

Two years ago, she'd hit the ground with a thud. It had taken one phone call from Kim DeLong. Until then, Joni had refused to believe the gossip about them. Kim had been Lowell's high school sweetheart, but they'd drifted apart in college. After marrying, then divorcing a banker in San Francisco, she'd returned to Viento del Mar a year earlier.

Judging by Kim's maliciously gleeful tone, she'd enjoyed calling Joni to crow about her affair with Lowell. She'd also enjoyed rubbing salt in the wound by saying that Joni had never been the right woman for him.

When confronted, Lowell had admitted the affair and,

furious about the phone call, dropped Kim immediately. Her bitterness was loud and abusive.

Joni pushed the memories aside. Kim and the divorce now seemed almost trivial compared with Lowell's death.

How was Jeff taking it? And what about Herb? The realization that she might have caused that dear man the worst kind of pain—the loss of his grandson—made her feel even more despondent.

Another thought sent terror prickling along Joni's spine. What if she were convicted of murder and sent to prison? She'd never even seen the inside of one except in films, the kind where prisoners were beaten and humiliated. How could she survive in a place like that?

And Jeff. What if he lost both his parents? Who would take care of him?

There was no other family but Herb, who was seventy-seven and had a heart condition. Joni's own father had deserted when she was just a child. Her mother, a hardworking waitress, had died of an aneurysm shortly after Joni turned eighteen.

Jeff's only other close relative was Lowell's brother, Dirk, whom she had met briefly at her wedding and at her father-in-law's funeral two years later. She remembered little about him except that he had bright blue eyes, like Jeff's, and seemed eager to get away from Viento del Mar.

At Lowell's request, Dirk had reluctantly donated sperm, but his only acknowledgement of Jeff was to send a small present each Christmas, usually an article of clothing that might have been chosen by his secretary. "Uncle" Dirk didn't even acknowledge the boy's birthday.

She and Lowell had discussed the possibility of some-

day telling Jeff the truth. Joni believed a child had a
right to know his own background, but Lowell had been
so uncomfortable with the subject that she'd put it aside
for later.

If she kept the secret too long, though, there was always the danger that Jeff might learn or suspect that he'd
been lied to. Rather than risk damaging his faith in her,
Joni meant to tell him the story when the time felt right.
But not now.

A tap at the door interrupted her reflections. "Joni?"
came a warm male voice.

Despite his gray hair and a few age spots, Herb Peterson retained the erect stature and classic face that had
once made him a popular figure in Viento del Mar society. The years had put a sparkle in his blue eyes and
lent a curve to his mouth, and the sight of him always
raised Joni's spirits.

Today, though, there was a redness around his eyelids
and a tightness to the way he held himself. She could
see that he had been mourning.

"Please come in." She gave him a quavery smile.

"The nurse said you could have visitors. Jeff's down
the hall looking at babies through a window," he said.
"I thought it might be best if you and I spoke alone."

She wished she knew the right thing to say. "Herb,
I'm so sorry about Lowell. I honestly don't remember
what happened."

"Did he attack you?" His voice broke painfully.

"He admitted he'd been watching me," she said.
"Then he took a step toward me. After that, I don't
remember anything."

Herb remained on the far side of the room. "I have
trouble accepting that my grandson was capable of stalking you. Let alone trying to harm you."

"I don't think he did, and yet he must have," Joni said. "It doesn't make sense, does it?"

"No, it doesn't. By the way, I caught a reporter trying to sneak in here. I told her I'd complain to her paper if she bothers you again."

"Thank you."

The town's newspaper and radio station were both owned by a local businessman who was an old friend of Herb's. The man couldn't ignore a major news story, but he would keep his staff within reasonable bounds.

A movement near the half-open door caught Joni's eye. She rolled her head on the pillow until she saw her son edging into the room. He wore his new navy pullover and tan Sunday-school pants, and his brown hair had been tamed with a comb and water. The extra tidy appearance only emphasized his unaccustomed pallor and the dark circles beneath his eyes.

"Hi, sweetie." She was grateful when he ran to her, even if his hug did make her ribs ache.

"Be careful, Jeff. Your mom's been hurt." Herb rested a hand atop his great-grandson's shoulder.

"What did you tell him about…about…?"

"He understands that his Dad's gone to heaven," Herb said. "We stopped by the church and prayed for him on our way here. I also asked the minister to officiate at the service."

Joni hadn't given a thought to the funeral. As Lowell's ex-wife and suspected slayer, she doubted she would have any say about the matter anyway. "That's fine. When will it be?"

"I've scheduled a memorial service for Monday afternoon," Herb said.

"Jeff?" She gazed into the storm-blue eyes of the

little boy who, despite a trace of gangliness, still seemed like her baby. "How are you feeling? Scared? Sad?"

"I miss Daddy," he admitted in a whisper. Although Lowell had rarely played with his son as a baby, he and Jeff had begun spending more time together since the divorce. "Do you think the police are wrong? Maybe he's not really dead but, like, in a coma."

"I'm afraid not, honey." Joni understood how he felt. She still imagined Lowell must be alive somewhere, out of sight. Working at the plant. Playing racquetball at the club.

"Maybe he could come back," Jeff persisted. "They could clone him. Like Mr. Spock on *Star Trek.*"

"That's make-believe," she said.

"I know," Jeff conceded.

He understood, Joni thought, at least on an eight-year-old level.

"When are you coming home, Mom?"

"The doctor said I might be able to leave tomorrow."

"I want you back today," the boy said.

"There could be some delay...." she began hesitantly. "Legal matters." She didn't know how to explain the possibility of her arrest. It might be more than Jeff could bear. Maybe more than she could bear, too.

"No, there won't," Herb said. "I've got the name of one of those top lawyers from Los Angeles. If anybody gives you a hard time, we'll talk to him."

"Herb, I can't afford that."

"I can," he said. "And I will. Don't you worry, Joni. Nothing can ever make up for losing my grandson, but I know in my heart you aren't to blame."

"Thank you," she whispered.

"It's a simple fact," he said. "No need for thanks."

The room fell silent. On a distant intercom, a woman's voice summoned a doctor to the delivery room.

Then Joni heard a noise in the hall that sent her heart slamming into her throat. It was irrational. A trick of the imagination.

Lowell's footsteps.

She knew that sound so well. The well-muscled weight of him. The confident step. The slight scuff as if he were kicking the ground out of his way.

She'd been listening to people come and go along the linoleum all day. Hospital personnel, patients, visitors. None of them had sounded remotely like Lowell.

The steps headed in their direction.

"That's Daddy." Jeff gave her a confused look, then ran toward the door.

Herb caught him by the arm. "Jeff, wait!"

"It's him!"

The newcomer stopped right outside, blocked by the partially closed door. Even though she knew that it couldn't possibly be Lowell, Joni found herself holding her breath.

The door swung open.

His hair was darker then Lowell's, and his eyes a deeper blue. But he had the same broad shoulders, the same arrogant stance.

To her surprise, she felt a shiver of the awe that used to run through her eleven years ago, every time Lowell stopped by her counter at the print shop. This man radiated an intense masculine power, perhaps even more strongly than his brother.

"Dirk," Herb said. "You got here fast. I just sent the message last night."

"I was in the Silicon Valley on business," said the man, giving his grandfather a rueful hug. "I'd been planning to head down this way tomorrow. Lowell and I were going to get together for the first time in years. Now we'll never have the chance, will we?''

As he turned toward Joni, his words seemed full of accusation. He paid no attention to Jeff.

In all these years, hadn't he ever been curious about the boy he'd fathered? What kind of man was Dirk Peterson?

In the past, it hadn't mattered. Now, it mattered tremendously. Because, Joni realized with a jolt, he might be in a position to take Jeff away from her.

Chapter Three

With a bandage wrapped around her head and her hair limp against the pillow, Joni didn't look much like the girl Dirk remembered from years ago.

She'd made a striking bride with her unusual bone structure and large hazel eyes. Her shy way of ducking her head had been countered by the athletic buoyancy with which she moved.

The impression of vulnerability mixed with resilience had lingered in Dirk's mind as he returned to the Los Angeles university where he'd been earning a business degree. But he'd been too preoccupied with his own unresolved adolescent rage and with deciding on a career to give much thought to the woman who married his domineering brother.

A few years later at his father's funeral, Joni had appeared very young in her black suit. But Dirk hadn't paid her much attention; he'd been suffering deep regret at the realization that he and his father would never have a chance to be close.

His sister-in-law looked older now, and less impressionable. In her expression, he read sorrow and determination.

She'd only grown more alluring, even in bandages, he

reflected unwillingly. She reminded him of a kitten that
had survived to maturity, gaining a few scars but developing a self-contained silkiness along the way.

He suspected she would always hold part of herself
back. That had been his impression when he first saw
her, dancing with his brother at the country club a few
nights before the wedding. It had been Lowell who
pulled her closer, Lowell who whispered in her ear, and
Joni who shifted her face subtly away.

What had her motives been in marrying his brother,
and then in divorcing him? Was she an opportunist? A
manipulator? Or simply an intriguing woman with hidden depths?

Dirk had to remind himself that this wasn't his battle
to fight.

The hell it wasn't. Lowell had been his brother even
though they'd come close to hating each other in their
younger years. Correction: Dirk had come close to hating the older sibling who delighted in taunting and belittling him.

There'd been one night when he'd nearly killed Lowell himself. It was just before Dirk went off to college,
and even now he could taste the hot fury as he'd
slammed his fist into his brother's jaw. Thank goodness
someone had pulled them apart. But after that, they'd
both known enough to keep their distance.

Now, when they'd finally been on the verge of reestablishing their relationship, maybe even doing some
business together, the chance had slipped away tragically—ripped away forever by the woman lying in front
of him.

The silence lengthened. Dirk roused himself to offer,
"I hope you're feeling better."

"The doctor says I'll be fine." She had a low, sensuous voice. "I was lucky."

Judging by her bandages, she must be in a lot of pain. That she refused to make a show of her discomfort fitted his impression of her reticent nature.

He needed some answers, though. And the sooner the better. "It would help if I knew exactly what my brother did. It's hard to mourn him properly when I have so many questions."

"I wish I could remember." Joni's eyes fixed on him earnestly. Brown flecks stood out against the green.

"The police said you have amnesia about the moments just before you were knocked unconscious. That isn't unusual."

Sometimes, he knew, amnesia could result from the brain's lack of time to transfer impressions into long-term memory before blacking out, in which case the information was lost forever. Other times, trauma made the victim repress the incident, in which case she might have a chance of remembering.

"You talked to the cops?" she asked.

"I don't like getting my information secondhand," Dirk said by way of confirmation.

After reading the newspaper this morning, he'd called the detective, who grudgingly answered a few questions. The police considered the case open-and-shut and, perhaps as a result, their work had been sloppy.

Dirk had taken some police-science courses in college and later undergone antiterrorist training while working for an overseas security agency. Even his current highly successful company, which developed new businesses in emerging economies, required attention to security.

He objected to the way the crime scene at Joni's house had been muddied with footprints. Furthermore, her clothes, on which the blood spatter might indicate where she'd stood during the stabbing, hadn't been collected until they'd been removed at the hospital. By then, spilled hummingbird nectar, rain and careless handling had smeared everything.

The officers had talked to the neighbors immediately adjacent, but they hadn't canvassed beyond that. Someone else might have noticed a jogger or an unfamiliar car but, without being questioned, wouldn't connect it to the case.

Despite the flaws in the police work, however, Dirk didn't doubt their conclusion. Lowell had been stalking Joni and she'd fought back.

The only issue that might have to be resolved by a jury was whether Lowell had presented an imminent threat to her life. Or had she simply seized the excuse to get rid of him?

"Did they tell you anything that wasn't in the paper?" she pressed.

He shrugged. "Not really." It was the truth, as far as it went.

"I'm not sure we should discuss this in present company." Herb tilted his head toward the boy, then changed the subject smoothly. "I apologize for calling your secretary, Dirk. I would have preferred to talk to you in person, but no one answered at your Rome apartment."

"That's because I'm hardly ever home. I'm the one who should apologize for not giving you my cell phone number," Dirk said.

He spent much of his time traveling. His company worked with venture capitalists and businesses seeking to expand into emerging nations. Using the Internet, contacts and financial sources, Dirk would identify locales with underutilized natural and human resources, and with reasonable political stability.

He then visited the sites, met with local officials and business people and prepared a report on the suitability of establishing manufacturing, mining, distribution or other operations. Depending on the client's needs, Dirk and his staff sometimes helped negotiate licenses and locate headquarters.

The work was exhilarating and highly profitable, but he shouldn't have let it become so all-consuming. He'd last seen his grandfather four years ago, when they'd spent several days together in Athens after Herb took a cruise of the Greek islands. Since then, contact had come mostly via Christmas cards.

Now he noticed a few more wrinkles on his grandfather's forehead and a bit of thinning in the gray hair. The man hadn't lost an ounce of his steely directness, though. "I'll take that cell phone number before you forget, grandson."

Dirk smiled. "You bet. I want us to get together a lot more often." He pulled out a business card and wrote the number on the back.

"You walk like Daddy," said the boy who stood next to Herb. "I thought you were him."

"You must be Jeff." Dirk bent and shook his hand solemnly, admiring the child's composure. It had to be tough on the boy to lose his father and to see his mother injured this way.

He was glad Lowell had been able to have his own son after all. Dirk hadn't been happy about his brother's demand that he donate sperm, but he'd been working on a dangerous assignment in central Asia and agreed to leave a specimen in case he was killed. When Lowell tersely notified him six months later that the sperm hadn't been needed, the news had come as a relief.

He wasn't ready to be a daddy. He wasn't even sure he was ready to take on the responsibilities of an uncle, but the circumstances left him no choice.

"Are you going to live here now?" Jeff asked.

"Just while I put some things in order," Dirk said.

"Who's going to take me to ball games?" Tears glistened in the little boy's eyes. "Daddy bought season tickets."

"Ball games?" Viento del Mar didn't have any professional teams. "Where?"

"Lowell sometimes took him to Los Angeles," Joni explained. "On their weekends together."

"I'll do it." Herb's fierce expression forestalled any attempt to point out that he was in no condition to be making a round-trip drive of more than four hours. "Don't you worry, Jeff."

The baseball issue could be handled later, Dirk decided. It was time to cut to the chase.

To Joni, he said, "I spoke to the family lawyer this morning. Are you aware that, in his will, Lowell left the printing company and the house half to me and half in trust for your son?"

Her lips formed the word. "No."

"The rest of the estate goes into a trust fund for Jeff," he said. "My brother named me as trustee."

"Who's going to run the company?" Herb asked. "I nearly drove myself into an early grave when I was in charge, and even so, I wasn't half the manager my son was, or Lowell, either. I'm not about to pick up the reins now."

"I can get it in shape to sell," Dirk said. "Or I can hire an executive to run it. Either way is all right with me. I think Jeff's mother ought to have some say in the matter."

Joni's long lashes drifted down, and she forced them up with a visible effort. "I can't make any decisions right now."

"It can wait," Dirk said. "Your first priority is to get well."

He wondered at the impulse he felt to protect her. He'd been aware all morning, through his meetings with the detective and the lawyer, that he'd been looking out for her interest as well as his nephew's.

Now the pallor of Joni's skin and the suffering in her gaze galvanized him. He wanted to reassure her that he would take care of everything so the tension could ease from her body and that lovely mouth would curve invitingly.

Yet he couldn't be sure she hadn't deliberately killed his brother. And even if he were, he didn't want to encourage her to depend on him. He wouldn't be staying in Viento del Mar long enough to do more than tie up loose ends.

"Call me in the morning and let me know what time they're releasing you," Herb said. "We'll pick you up."

Joni shook her head on the pillow. "I'll take a cab."

"Don't be ridiculous!" Herb said, bristling.

His grandfather must care a great deal about this woman, Dirk thought in surprise. Even Lowell's death hadn't shaken their bond.

"I'm not being ridiculous," Joni said. "You know me, Herb. When I'm hurt, I'm like a wild animal. I hole up and lick my wounds." She gave a small shrug. "I just need some time alone."

"You've spent too much time alone after my grandson—" Herb glanced at Jeff "—did what he did with Kim. I won't let you bear this by yourself."

"You can come over later," Joni said. "I'll call you after I've gotten my bearings. I promise."

Herb grumbled but gave in. "I reserve the right to spoil my great-grandson rotten in the meantime."

"By all means." Warmth suffused the woman's face, and the entire room seemed to glow. Whatever else might be true of her, she clearly loved her son.

Dirk glanced at the boy. This was not only his nephew but, except for Herb, his only close relative.

He could see his brother in the boy's build, but that didn't explain Dirk's pang of recognition. With a jolt, he realized the boy reminded him of himself. The troubled deep blue eyes. The unruly hair, darker than either Lowell's or Joni's.

No, not himself, he thought sternly, but his mother. Tina Peterson, who had died of lupus when he was twelve, had been the source of Dirk's dramatic coloring. In Lowell, those genes must have skipped a generation.

Herb clapped a hand onto the boy's shoulder. "We'll let you get some rest, Joni. See you tomorrow."

"Bye, Herb. Jeff, I love you." Her gaze flicked toward Dirk. "It's good to see you, although I'm sorry about the circumstances."

"So am I." He let the older man and the boy precede him through the door.

He disliked leaving Joni in the hospital unguarded. Yet if she had slain his brother for her own advantage, the person she would most need guarding against was Dirk himself.

"Join us for supper?" Herb asked as they descended in the elevator.

"Sure," he said. "At the club?"

"Our special club," his grandfather replied. "Follow us."

Outside, the clouds were clearing. In the twilight, Herb's bright red sports car whipped out of the parking lot ahead of the blue rented Volvo.

Dirk had chosen the solidly built car out of habit, after years of working in developing nations where the dangers ranged from gun-wielding rebels to vicious potholes. He had to smile at the way he and his grandfather had reversed the traditional roles. Herb had youthful fervor to spare.

Herb and Jeff's "club" turned out to be McDonald's. The boy ordered a Happy Meal but barely ate half, then wandered dispiritedly toward the brightly colored play area.

"Usually he runs so fast he's a blur," Herb said. "He seemed to take the news okay about his father, but I know he's hurting."

"Want to leave?"

"We need to talk first." His grandfather cleared his throat and leaned forward. "I want you to clear your brother's name. I don't believe he attacked Joni."

"I thought you liked her." Dirk speared a French fry.

"I more than like her. I love that girl." The older man swallowed hard. "She's like the daughter I never had."

"Either she murdered Lowell, or he tried to murder her," Dirk said. "I can't clear one without condemning the other."

"There has to be some other explanation," Herb insisted.

"The police will—"

"This is Viento del Mar!" Herb smacked his cup onto the table so hard it sent droplets flying. "What do they know about investigating a homicide? Besides, you're the only one who can get inside Lowell's head. Try to figure out what he was doing and thinking this past month, why he would resume harassing Joni just when they were on good terms again.''

Dirk wanted to help, but he couldn't deliver the impossible. ''Grandpa, I'm not a mind reader.''

''Maybe he had a mental disorder or was taking some medication that affected his behavior. There has to be a reason!''

Dirk was on the verge of protesting the urgency of returning to business when something stopped him. It might have been the pinched look on his grandfather's face. It might have been the notion that, in spite of their long-standing antagonism, he owed his brother something.

But fundamentally, it was the realization that the main reason he itched to leave Viento del Mar was that, since the moment he'd returned, the old anger and pain had closed around him like a vise.

Dirk had never been able to please his overcritical father, Donald. In his father's view, he wasn't athletic enough; he was too intellectual; he picked the wrong friends.

Glib and popular, Lowell had adopted his father's attitude. At the country club, at school, in front of friends, he never missed a chance to put his little brother in his place.

With his rebellious streak, Dirk had maintained a tough exterior. Inside, there were moments when he ached so much he could hardly breathe. The worst times were when he needed his father most. After his mother's death. After the breakup of his first intense teenage love affair. Whenever he felt vulnerable, that was when Donald tried hardest to reshape him and Lowell was at his most supercilious.

Well, Dirk wasn't a kid anymore. This request meant a lot to his grandfather. It was time to face down the old emotions and defuse what was left of them.

That he might also be helping Joni shouldn't have affected his decision. But when he pictured her lying in the hospital bed, pale and injured, Dirk understood how helpless she must feel. He just hoped he wasn't giving her too much benefit of the doubt. There was no sympathy in his heart for liars and schemers.

"All right," he told his grandfather. "I'll do the best I can. But you may not like what I find."

"As long as it's the truth," Herb said, "I'll take it."

HOSPITAL POLICY REQUIRED that departing patients be wheelchaired to the front door by a volunteer. On her way out on Friday morning, Joni had intended to stop by the public relations office to collect her undelivered plant, but it was out of the way and she hated to inconvenience the volunteer.

She hoped to return to work on Monday. If Basil gave it a good watering today, she told herself, the plant should survive until then.

As planned, she took a cab home. It was a clear, crisp day, and the driver, a man in his fifties, maneuvered the hospital's steep drive so carefully that the car barely jounced.

Joni's ribs and head didn't hurt much, thanks to a last dose of hospital painkillers. The doctor who removed her bandages that morning had given her a prescription, which lay unfilled in her purse.

She didn't want to take any medication that might blur her thinking. If it were possible, she needed to recall those final moments of Lowell's life. She needed to clear her name, not only with the police but with Dirk, as well. For some reason, it mattered very much what he thought.

He had the same brooding intensity as his brother, but there was a gentleness about him that touched her. Several times, she'd even imagined she saw concern in his expression.

She knew better, however, than to yield to her instinctive physical response to the man. He possessed the same magnetism that had drawn her to Lowell, and look where that had led.

The route home took them past Peterson Printing. It lay a couple of miles east of the hospital along San Bernardo Road, one of the town's two main streets. The original one-story building in front didn't look like much. Signs advertising photocopying and low-cost faxes plastered the front window through which Joni could see the counter where she'd been working eleven years ago when she met Lowell.

A stand of trees partially masked the much larger building in back. Inside could be found the massive presses that thundered day and night, the bustling art department, the layout and typesetting computers, the photoreproduction and engraving equipment, the binding facility, the warehouse and loading dock and, of course, the offices.

The local newspaper was printed here. So were wedding invitations, magazines, books, advertisements, corporate annual statements and other orders from around the region. She could almost hear the roar of the presses and smell the tang of the ink. It had been exciting to work there, especially after she learned desktop publishing and was promoted from clerking. Although she'd given up college after marrying, Joni had continued at her job until Jeff was born.

Lowell would have preferred that she spend her days swimming and playing tennis at the country club rather than working. He'd disapproved of her in other ways, too: her lack of style, her shyness, her tendency to get disheveled while playing with Jeff.

Nothing that came naturally to Joni seemed to please him. In time, she'd realized that even when she did win his acceptance, it was only temporary. To survive emotionally, she'd had to stop caring about his opinion.

The cab turned into Canyon Acres, the meandering development where she lived. Because of the uneven terrain, the homes were widely spaced below the forested hills. Some of the lower slopes blazed pink with bougainvillea, while each house sported its own emerald patch of lawn.

"Say, wasn't there a murder out here?" the cabbie asked as he turned into Joni's cul-de-sac.

She didn't want to reveal too much to a stranger. "Somewhere around here."

"You be careful, lady." He pulled into her driveway and stopped. "You want me to walk you inside?"

Her stalker was dead. What did she have to fear? "No, thanks," Joni said.

"I'll wait out here while you take a look around." The man had a kind face. "You wave at me out the door, and I'll go."

"Thank you." A surge of relief caught Joni off guard. She hadn't realized she would feel this nervous about returning to the scene of the tragedy.

Maybe it hadn't been such a good idea to come home by herself. Still, although she knew most people would have opted for companionship, she had grown up spend-

ing time alone and needed a certain amount of solitude
to feel complete.

Joni paid and got out of the cab. Thank goodness the
police had brought her purse to the hospital Wednesday
night after locking the house, she reflected as she took
out her keys.

On the porch, she scooped up two newspapers and
plucked a bill from the mailbox. As she unlocked the
door, she listened for anything amiss, but heard only the
hum of the refrigerator.

She checked the living room, the den and the bed-
rooms. Drawers stood partially open and cushions had
been tossed aside by the police, to whom she'd given
permission to enter the premises. Detective MacDougall
had told her that he'd tried to minimize the mess.

In the kitchen, she found masculine footprints smeared
as if someone had tried to wipe up mud with a paper
towel. Too stiff even to contemplate washing the floor,
she returned to the front and signaled the driver.

After he pulled away, Joni changed from the slacks
and blouse that Kathryn had brought into jeans and a
rose-colored sweater. Then, gathering her courage, she
went out the back door.

Chapter Four

Sagging yellow police tape surrounded the patio. Against a support beam leaned Jeff's bike, the front spokes indented where Joni had fallen on them. She wanted to put it away but decided not to enter the crime scene.

Someone had collected the broken glass, and yesterday's heavy rain must have washed the blood off the concrete. The glass table stood sideways to its usual position; the small barbecue grill remained close to the house, by the back door. Brown patches staining the edges of the narrow lawn were the only reminder of the tragedy that had taken place here two days before.

Snatches of memory came to her from that night: the wind and the darkness, the gash of fear when Lowell confronted her. Was it possible she had stabbed him? Could a person commit such a violent act and not remember it?

In high school, she had refused to dissect a frog because the idea of cutting into an animal, even a dead one, distressed her. Could she have cut down a man?

Joni tried to recapture the tactile sense of the haft in her hand, but she couldn't. The only way she could picture herself using a knife was against a cutting board.

Trembling, she retreated inside. At least she'd gotten through this first agonizing visit to the backyard. Surely her anxiety would fade with time. If not, she could sell the house. But that would mean a disruption for Jeff, and it would be expensive. Regardless of what anyone might think about her wanting to get her hands on the inheritance, she intended to preserve every penny for her son.

Twinges of pain crackled through her ribs. In the bathroom, Joni took a couple of over-the-counter pain pills and forced herself to confront the bruised face in the mirror.

Dark circles made half-moons beneath her hazel eyes, and her skin had a raw pallor, as if she hadn't slept in a week. Although she'd never been vain, Joni applied some cosmetics to cover the worst damage.

Bending forward, she fought an onrush of dizziness as she brushed her shoulder-length blond hair into its accustomed bun. The brush grazed the swelling on one side, and she winced.

At least she no longer looked as if she'd put on fright makeup for Halloween, she decided, and dampened her bangs so they would lie straight. Next, she headed for the kitchen to fix some coffee.

Joni had read yesterday's newspaper at the hospital, so she chucked that one into the recycle bin. Opening today's edition, she sat down to face the worst.

A follow-up story offered no new information, just sorrowful reactions by leading citizens and employees at Peterson Printing. As for Joni herself, a hospital spokesman—her boss, Basil—reported that she was recovering.

Gee, she was in good condition. That should come as welcome news to her rib cage.

She skimmed the rest of the newspaper, stopping to

read a short article about the soccer league. A group picture of volunteers included Jeff's coach, Charlie Rogers. How normal they all looked. And what a nice change it was to read about something that didn't involve Lowell's death.

Charlie wasn't a bad-looking man, she decided as she studied the photograph. He'd been thoughtful to bring the flowers, but she felt no particular attraction to him. In fact, she hadn't been attracted to anyone in a long time, not until yesterday.

Into her mind leaped an image of Dirk, probing and intensely masculine. In the hospital, his nearness had made her sharply aware of her own femininity. She'd had to force herself not to drink in the rugged length of him, the tanned skin and thick, barely tamed dark hair. Not to let her gaze linger on the sturdy hands as they tapped impatiently against his thigh.

With a start, Joni realized she had been disappointed when he left without touching her. He hadn't brushed a wisp of hair off her forehead or even shaken her hand. She wanted him to touch her. This stranger. This man who held the power to devastate her world. She must have been alone too long, she reflected with a sigh.

Her glance returned to the newspaper photo. Soccer. Tomorrow was Saturday, which meant Jeff must have a game. She needed to call Kathryn to confirm the time and place.

Joni pressed a rapid-dial button on her phone, preset to the Owenses' number. On the third ring, Fred answered. He ran his life insurance business from a home office.

"Joni?" he said when he heard her voice. "Are you out of the hospital?"

"So rumor has it."

"Kathryn or I would be happy to bring you some lunch," he offered.

"No, thanks. But I do need to know about the game tomorrow."

"Eleven o'clock at the high school," he said. "Do you want us to take Jeff?"

"Thanks, but I want to keep things as normal as possible for him." She brushed aside the thought that it would be a relief not to have to attend. "Or maybe I should keep him home till he's had more time to adjust. What do you think?"

There was a pause while Fred weighed his answer. She knew how much he valued sports; if it hadn't been for a knee injury, he might have played professional baseball himself.

"If he strongly doesn't want to go, I wouldn't force him," Bobby's father said at last. "But otherwise, kids do their grieving in bits and pieces over a long period. Keeping him home might even delay his adjustment."

"That's what I think, too," Joni agreed. "Thanks, Fred."

"If there's anything you need, just call."

After she hung up, she sat in the kitchen trying to settle her uneasy spirits. What was it that kept nagging at her as if she'd left some business unfinished?

Through the partly open blinds, she regarded the rosebushes below the retaining wall that separated her narrow yard from the hill. One branch hung limply, probably broken either by the police or by Lowell himself.

On the slope above, just past a yellow-flowered bush, a squirrel scampered across a large gray rock. It was a peaceful, almost idyllic scene.

What could she have overlooked? There must be some

clue about what had happened, something that would jog her memory.

Joni studied the calendar hanging beside the refrigerator. Halloween was next Thursday. It would also be her thirtieth birthday, not an occasion she looked forward to with much joy.

Especially with a possible murder charge hanging over her head.

Determined not to brood, she carried her cup to the sink. As she set it down, she caught sight of the cutlery block with its telltale empty slot. Joni's stomach clenched. She should put the blasted thing out of sight. But right now, she couldn't bring herself to touch it.

Grimly, she opened the dishwasher and set her cup in the top rack. The thing was nearly full, so after pouring some detergent into the dispenser, she turned it on.

Outside, clouds dimmed the sunlight. Weariness came over Joni so swiftly that she barely managed to stagger to the den before collapsing on the couch. She felt lightheaded, perhaps from the delayed effects of hospital medication or from the injury itself. Before she knew it, she was asleep.

In her dreams, her mind must have been working. When she awoke, she had a sharp, disturbing realization of what she had missed.

The dishwasher.

Groggily, Joni stumbled to her feet and went into the kitchen. Finished with sudsing, the machine was rumbling into a rinse cycle. Heedless of the spray, she yanked it open. A second later, the water was automatically cut off.

Her gaze went first to the cutlery rack in the bottom, but there was nothing unusual about the welter of forks and spoons and butter knives. Her throat tightening, Joni pulled out the top rack.

There it lay, barely noticeable behind a row of glasses. The carving knife missing from her block.

She had laid it flat because it was too long to fit with the regular cutlery. It was such an ordinary sight that it hadn't even registered in her conscious mind, and the police must not have thought to check the top rack.

The weapon they'd found in her hand wasn't hers. Whom did it belong to, and how had it gotten there?

Numbly, Joni set her find on the counter, then closed the dishwasher. It sluiced back into action.

Water on the floor was turning the policemen's dried footprints into a muddy mess. From force of habit, she grabbed a rag from beneath the sink and knelt to wipe it up. The routine act of scrubbing freed her mind to absorb the significance of her discovery. She hadn't killed Lowell.

The knowledge came with a flood of relief. She hadn't deprived Herb of his grandson, hadn't cheated Jeff of his father and hadn't taken the life of a man whom, in spite of everything, she still cared about.

She hadn't killed him, but someone had. Someone who was walking around, unsuspected. Someone who had tried to pass the blame off on her.

Would the police believe her story? A person could probably pick up a similar knife at a thrift shop or garage sale, not to mention any department store. If only she hadn't washed the darn thing, it would have been easier to prove that her own knife had been sitting here for two days with food on it.

She tossed the rag into the sink and Joni sank into a chair at the table. She was too lost in thought to notice that a car had stopped in the driveway. Only when the doorbell rang did she jerk back into the present.

It might be Herb and Jeff. Or the mail carrier with a package. Or...

The killer. He could be anyone.

The bell shrilled again. She didn't move.

Someone tried the knob. In disbelief, Joni heard it turn and the door creak open.

She must have forgotten to lock it after she waved to the cabdriver. "Herb?" she tried to say, but the words stuck in her throat.

The visitor didn't call out. It was strange the way he walked into her house unannounced. She heard masculine footsteps marching through the hallway. Crossing the den.

Maybe she should run for the phone or grab a knife or...

It was too late. Someone was coming through the kitchen door.

DIRK FOLLOWED Terry MacDougall through a rabbit warren of desks and cubbyholes to a partitioned bay brightened by a view of the police department parking lot. Files, foam cups and While You Were Out messages littered the desk.

"Sit anywhere," the detective said.

Aside from his own swivel chair, two mismatched high-back seats crammed the small space. Computer printouts filled both of them. Dirk looked to see if the man was joking, noted that he wasn't and shifted a stack of papers onto the floor.

"You understand," the detective went on, "that department procedure won't allow me to tell you much."

Dealing with the authorities in Viento del Mar wasn't

much different from negotiating with officials in a Third World country, Dirk mused as he sat down. The main differences were that he doubted Detective MacDougall expected a bribe and there were no naked electrical lines snaking along the wall.

"As you know, I've cleared this with the chief," Dirk said. "He seemed sympathetic to my position."

MacDougall regarded him with open cynicism. In his late fifties, the man had thinning, light brown hair and a few acne scars left from adolescence. He'd spent a lot of years on the force, Dirk guessed, and even in a small town had probably seen too much for his own good.

"Of course he did. The Petersons own one of the biggest companies in town, as I'm sure you reminded him." Idly, the detective adjusted a triptych of photographs facing him. His family, Dirk assumed. "I suppose you think your brother's death rates special treatment."

"'Special treatment' meaning what? I don't expect you to blow my nose for me or wipe the widow's tears. I also don't expect you guys to be in a hurry to name a suspect so you'll look good in the newspapers." Seeing anger flare in those pale eyes, Dirk added, "Nothing personal, Detective."

MacDougall shrugged. "Seems pretty obvious what happened. The only question is, was she really in fear of her life? That's the D.A.'s job to decide."

"Is that your idea of detective work—to settle for what seems obvious?" Dirk demanded, and immediately realized he'd gone too far. "I'm sorry. I realize you're the professional here. But I don't think you can write this case off that easily."

The other man quirked an eyebrow. "Mind if I ask why you're so keen on helping your sister-in-law?"

No point in explaining about his promise to Herb.

Dirk doubted the detective would take kindly to the idea of his conducting a private investigation.

Yesterday afternoon, he had questioned his brother's doctor about any mood disorders or medications. No luck there, not even a referral to a counselor during the divorce. Lowell would have considered it a weakness to seek help with his emotions.

Earlier today, Dirk had gone through his brother's office at the plant but found nothing that hinted at Lowell's state of mind. The police had already searched there as well as Lowell's house, his car and his club locker, but so far as Dirk knew, they hadn't found anything.

He planned to talk to his brother's friends at the country club, especially Kim DeLong, who he understood was bitter that Lowell had ended their affair instead of marrying her. It wasn't an interview he looked forward to.

"She isn't just my sister-in-law," Dirk said. "She's also my nephew's mother. Even if Joni is eventually cleared, what will the strain and publicity of a trial do to Jeff in the meantime? I think subjecting either of them to unnecessary prosecution would be reprehensible."

"Are you so sure it's unnecessary?"

"Think about it, Detective," he said. "There are no witnesses, and it's medically credible that Joni doesn't remember what happened. Even if she did stab my brother, which is by no means proven, doesn't the evidence point overwhelmingly to self-defense?"

"I'd say a jury should decide that for themselves." MacDougall watched him intently.

"These aren't cardboard figures on a TV show," Dirk pressed. "My sister-in-law has been through a lot already. So has my nephew. A trial isn't exactly a minor stress, and it could last a long time. I don't think that's a step to be taken lightly."

"What are you asking me to do?" The man fiddled again with the photo frames. Dirk glimpsed one of the shots, a middle-aged woman posing with two teenage girls. So the detective *did* have a family.

"Don't be in a rush to go to the D.A.," he said. "Talk to people around the neighborhood. Look into whether anyone might have had a grudge against my brother or my sister-in-law."

MacDougall grimaced. "I hate to tell you this, Peterson, but I don't think we're going to get any new evidence in this case."

"Maybe not, but what's your rush?" Dirk challenged. "If you miss anything, it could prove highly embarrassing. I should think you'd want to cross every *t* and dot every *i*."

A sigh escaped the other man. "Fine. I'll hold off for a few days while we do some more legwork. That's the best I can offer."

"Good enough." Dirk stood, and they shook hands.

The other man's grip was damp but firm. He handed over a card. "That's my home number. Don't use it unless you have to."

"Thanks."

On his way out, Dirk passed Communications and heard a dispatcher summoning an officer to the scene of a two-car collision. It made him wonder what his life would be like if he'd yielded to impulse in college and switched his major from business to police science.

Still angry at Lowell after their knockdown fight and largely alienated from his father, Donald, Dirk had considered breaking with his family's expectations and pursuing a career in law enforcement. He'd taken some courses in the field and found he liked the subject but disliked the prospect of being confined to routine police work.

He'd stuck with business. Then, during his senior year, a buddy in Dirk's martial arts club told him of a firm recruiting for overseas security work.

On impulse, Dirk went with him to the recruiter's presentation and got hooked. He'd signed up immediately after graduation, working as a bodyguard and, later, as a consultant assessing security needs for American businesses.

He didn't regret the decision, although the work had been more grueling and less romantic than he'd imagined. It was during those years that he'd identified a need for his present consulting business, and had capitalized on the knowledge and contacts he'd acquired.

Dirk only wished that either he'd never met Elena or that he could have saved her. Maybe she would have died even if she'd never fallen in love with him. But that possibility didn't make it hurt less. He couldn't help her now. Regrets accomplished nothing, Dirk reflected, and pushed them aside.

After leaving the police station, he stopped for a hamburger, then drove to his grandfather's condo. There he found Herb washing the lunch dishes and looking tired after a morning of playing with Jeff.

Joni hadn't called yet, but brushing aside any objections, Dirk insisted on driving his nephew home. The boy collected an overnight bag and got into the front seat. After fastening his seat belt, he sat up straight, arms wrapped around the bag. Jeff had the strong Peterson jaw, Dirk noticed, and Joni's well-defined mouth, but the innocent gaze of a little boy.

As he started the car, he wondered what they could

talk about. Dirk had dealt with officials from Beirut to Bangkok, but eight-year-olds were another matter. Until now, Jeff had been nothing more than a name and a picture on a Christmas card.

"What grade are you in?" he asked.

"Third." The boy stared through the windshield.

"What are you studying?"

"Cursive."

"They teach cursing in school?" Dirk turned left from Canyon Vista onto San Bernardo Road.

"No, that's writing instead of printing!" The boy must have seen his smile. "You're being silly, aren't you?"

"I'm trying."

"That's funny," the boy said.

"Then why aren't you laughing?"

"I mean, it's funny that you made a joke," Jeff explained. "Dad never made jokes, just Mom."

Lowell wasn't known for his sense of humor, Dirk had to admit. "Do you expect me to be exactly like your father just because I'm his brother?"

"I don't know," Jeff said wistfully. "I don't have a brother. If I did, I think he'd be like me."

"You can never tell." They went by the printing plant and crossed the bridge over Viento del Mar Creek. Following the map his grandfather had drawn, Dirk passed the high school and turned into the Canyon Acres development. "Can you help me find your street?"

"Sure." The boy proceeded to give clear directions, sounding very grown up.

Dirk wondered why he felt so intrigued by his nephew. Maybe it was because, with his bright turquoise eyes, Jeff seemed almost a mirror image of what Dirk had been like at his age.

"I wonder who that is." Jeff pointed to a maroon sedan parked in a driveway. Startled, Dirk realized they'd reached Joni's house, which was set partway up a hill.

He parked by the curb. "You don't recognize it?"

The boy shook his head, then indicated the open front door. "Mom never leaves the door like that. Flies could get in."

Disquieted, Dirk slid from the car. Jeff hopped out beside him. He didn't want to call the police without good reason. Still, the situation didn't look right, and with her injuries, Joni was especially vulnerable.

He couldn't leave Jeff in the car while he investigated, though. The safest place would be with him.

"Stay behind me," Dirk said, and the boy obeyed. In single file, they walked toward the house.

Chapter Five

The footsteps grew louder. Whoever had invaded Joni's home was in the den, almost at the kitchen....

The lanky figure of her boss appeared in the doorway. "There you are," he said.

"Basil!" Joni nearly chuckled in relief, except that the sallow skin and shadowed gray eyes of the public relations director evoked solemnity rather than amusement. "You didn't have to do this."

"The staff would never forgive me if I didn't give you this." He held out a purple chrysanthemum plant.

"Thanks. It's lovely," she said. "I'll just set it on the table." He handed it over without speaking.

With his long silences and elliptical comments, Joni's boss wasn't exactly Mr. Personality, but she liked him. And she respected his ongoing struggle as a recovering alcoholic.

She knew it was up to her to keep the conversation going. "I heard you trying to get past the nurse at the hospital. She certainly put her foot down."

"She was just doing her job." Expressionless, he gazed around the kitchen.

"I'm going to try to come back to work on Monday."

"That would be fine."

Seconds ticked by on the wall clock. Before she could think of anything else to say, Joni heard a rapid, light tapping at the back door. With relief, she recognized the knock as Celia Lu's.

"My neighbor." She went to answer it. After a moment's pause, Basil followed.

"You are home!" The dark-haired woman patted Joni's shoulder and edged by her into the utility hall. "I come in? Oh, who is this?"

Joni made introductions. Basil gave Celia's hand a perfunctory shake and the two stood eyeing each other like a pair of dogs both trying to stake out the same territory.

"Joni needs to rest," Basil growled at last.

"I think, if she needs something, maybe I can help!" Celia chirped. Ignoring the man's fidgeting, she plied Joni with questions about the hospital and the doctor's orders and the police investigation.

They sat in the living room, listening to her account of what had happened, but she had nothing new to offer. If a third person had been involved, Celia hadn't seen him.

On the street, a car stopped. Joni had her back to the window and didn't realize anyone was approaching the house until Celia said, "It's your son. And a handsome man! Do I meet him before?"

"I certainly haven't," Basil growled. "Who is that?"

Joni turned and, through the translucent curtain panels, watched Dirk edge toward the house at an angle. A tan turtleneck sweater and tailored dark blue slacks emphasized the muscular contours of his chest and the slimness of his hips.

With the light behind him, he couldn't see them, Joni realized. "It's my brother-in-law."

Even if she hadn't known Dirk was trained to handle danger, it was obvious from the tight positioning of his arms and body and his repeated, quick scans of the area. Behind him, Jeff mimicked Dirk's movements, even cocking his head the same way. It was as if the two had spent years together.

"I didn't know," Celia said. "Lowell had a brother?"

"He lives overseas." Irrationally, Joni was glad Dirk had come. Just the sight of him made her feel safer.

"I'll be going, then." Basil stood up. "Don't let the chrysanthemum sit too long before planting. It'll get root bound."

He stomped outside, passed by the startled Dirk with barely a nod and headed for his car.

"A strange man," Celia said. "I hope he does not visit often."

"He won't need to. I plan to go back to work as soon as I can." Joni reached the front door as her son bounded up the steps. She caught him in a hug, which he accepted with less wiggling than usual.

"What was Mr. Dupont doing here?" Jeff asked from below her chin. "We thought it was a stranger! Why did you leave your door open? Oh, hello, Mrs. Lu."

Somehow Joni got through the next few minutes, making introductions and polite conversation until Celia reluctantly departed. Jeff wandered into the den to play video games.

Throughout the encounter, Dirk's eyes swept the living room as if it held a secret that he intended to extract from it. Concentration gave his face the intensity of a wolf's.

"You can't find my decor all that interesting," she said when they were alone.

"What?"

"I got most of this stuff at a thrift shop," Joni pointed out. "What's so fascinating?"

The corners of his mouth twitched. "I always inspect my surroundings. It pays to be alert."

"I know you do business in emerging nations, but surely they can't be that perilous! Not people's living rooms anyway."

He shifted on the balls of his feet like a wild creature uneasy at finding itself indoors. "Exposed electrical wires can kill. So can a snake in search of a dry place to sleep."

"What fun," Joni said dryly. "We don't have to contend with any of those threats around here, thank goodness."

He started to laugh, then sobered. The amusement evaporated from Joni's mood, too, as she realized the irony of her remark, given what had happened to Lowell.

That reminded her about the knife. She was accustomed to keeping her own counsel, but she didn't have enough experience to evaluate how she should handle this situation. Besides, Dirk of all people had a right to know the truth about his brother's slaying.

"I want to show you something," she said. "I need your advice."

"Mine?" A dark eyebrow quirked.

"Dirk, I don't know much about evidence. Or murder investigations."

He regarded her assessingly. "Are we playing helpless, Joni?"

The man certainly knew how to irritate her! "Is it playing coy to need a second opinion?"

She hadn't realized he was moving toward her until his muscular frame halted only inches away. "You could be trying to win me to your side. It's an old tactic, Joni. Ask my advice, and I may start to feel like we're allies.''

There was no point in beating around the bush with this man. "If we aren't allies, what are we?"

He grinned. "That's more like it."

"More like what?"

"The attitude I would expect from the woman who kicked my brother out when he did her wrong."

"I didn't kick him out," Joni admitted. "I kicked myself out. Otherwise, why would I be living with thrift-shop furniture while he kept the mansion?"

"You could have fought for it. Most women would have." Dirk reached out and brushed a long wisp of hair from her cheek. His touch was gentle and oddly possessive.

Joni wanted him to touch her again and wished she didn't. In her confusion, she spoke more forcefully than she'd intended. "I never felt comfortable in that house anyway. It belonged more to his housekeeper than it did to me."

"You might have insisted on a settlement. After all, you were the injured party," he pressed.

"Lowell provided for Jeff," she said.

"Yes, I know. He bought this house for him," Dirk said. "That was the only way you would accept it."

"You do very thorough research," she conceded.

"I hope so. Now show me your evidence."

There was no hint of indulgence in his tone, which was fine with Joni. She liked directness in a man. Even brutal honesty was better than manipulation.

Maybe that was why she'd put up with Lowell as long as she had. At least she knew where she stood with him even if that place wasn't particularly elevated. Or, rather, she'd believed she knew where she stood until the day Kim called.

"It's in the kitchen." She led the way, keenly aware of Dirk's heat radiating against her back.

The man had a gift for dominating his surroundings. Dirk might be less flashy than his brother, but he had more real strength.

No wonder the two hadn't gotten along. Lowell could never bear to be upstaged.

"There." Joni indicated the knife on the counter.

Dirk's lips pursed as he studied it, mentally measuring its size and design. "Where did you find it?"

"In the dishwasher." She clicked her tongue. "*After* I ran it. Stupid, huh?"

"The police should have checked."

"They probably did. It wasn't in the cutlery tray; it was half-hidden under some glasses. I didn't notice it myself until too late."

He scowled. "It's sloppy work, nevertheless."

"Maybe so, but that doesn't change the facts," she said. "Now that the knife's been washed, I'm going to have a hard time proving it's been sitting here all this time, aren't I?"

"Are these the only knives you have?" He indicated the cutlery block.

"No," she said. "I picked up a few odds and ends when I was living in an apartment, right after the separation."

"Where are they?"

She opened a drawer. "Here. But the police probably checked it when they went through the house."

As Dirk shifted past her, she caught the scent of expensive soap and, beneath it, a hint of something feral.

Without warning, prickles of desire ran along her skin and her nipples stiffened.

Joni didn't want to feel anything for this man and yet she found his nearness intensely pleasurable. So pleasurable that she had to back up several steps for her own peace of mind. From the den came the pings and screeches of a video game. The reminder of her son's presence brought her down to earth.

Dirk examined the contents of the drawer without handling anything. "Most of them are different makes, but there's a paring knife that's the same."

"It's the department store's house brand," she said. "Lots of people have them."

"So the murder weapon could have come from the drawer even if it didn't come from the block," he reasoned.

"I didn't have another knife that size," she protested, then had to add, "I don't think."

"You're not sure?"

"Not one hundred percent. But if I were in a hurry, I would've grabbed one out of the block, not poked around in a drawer."

His gaze returned to the knife on the counter. There was a long pause; she could almost see wheels turning inside his head as he mulled over the implications of this discovery. She tried to hold still, to give him time to think, but her head felt suddenly light. It had been foolish to remain standing this long, Joni realized as she caught hold of the counter to steady herself.

Dirk grasped her arm. "Have you eaten lunch?"

His face tilted down, his well-defined mouth inches from hers. At close range, the contrast between his thick dark hair and shocking blue eyes struck her as intensely sensual. If she weren't careful, she might lift her mouth and taste him.

Taking her by the shoulders, Dirk steered her to the table. Blurrily, Joni noticed that, by the wall clock, it was 1:35. "I had coffee."

"That's a great lunch. What do you plan to have for dinner—iced tea?" He opened the refrigerator and peered inside.

"I forget to eat sometimes," she admitted.

He removed a loaf of bread, a package of turkey slices and some condiments. "You don't think much of yourself, do you?"

"What is this, instant psychoanalysis?" Joni said, bristling. "Lots of people forget to eat."

"Lots of people don't also marry my brother." Pulling out a cutting board, Dirk set to work. "I loved the guy—hell, when I was a little kid, I practically worshiped him—but he could be a real pain. Herb told me how he put you down all the time."

She rested her chin on one palm. "We were a mismatch. I guess when he proposed, he saw something in me that wasn't there."

"He knew exactly what he was getting when he married you. Mustard?"

"Yes." She nodded distractedly. "What *was* he getting, since you seem to have it figured out?"

"A beautiful woman who thought so little of herself that she would put up with his arrogance," Dirk said. "Exactly what he needed, and not an easy combination to find."

"I'm not beautiful," Joni protested. "And I'm not a pushover, either. I didn't put up with his playing around."

"Kim DeLong forced the issue by phoning you."

Dirk layered tomato and lettuce onto the sandwich and sliced it into two triangles. "Is this enough food?"

"Plenty." As she accepted the plate, Joni discovered that she was ravenous. The glass of orange juice that Dirk handed her disappeared almost as fast as the sandwich.

What he'd said about Lowell rang true, although it bothered her that this stranger had more insight into her marriage than she did. Still, Dirk had known his brother a lot longer.

"About the knife." He straddled a chair next to her. "You'll need to give it to the police as soon as possible."

"Even though it won't do any good?"

"It could help your lawyer create doubt about your guilt," he suggested.

His words echoed through her mind with eerie unreality. Legalistic maneuverings sounded so foreign to her ordinary life. "Do you know if they're going to file charges?"

Dirk tapped one finger on the surface of the table. "I hope not."

"Because you think I'm innocent, or to spare Jeff?" Joni caught her breath. Why had she brought up the delicate subject of their son?

"Herb asked me to find out what really happened, for Lowell's sake," he said quietly. "And I guess for Jeff's sake, too."

Jeff's, but not hers. "Does Herb think I might have killed Lowell on purpose?"

"My grandfather loves you," Dirk said. "Therefore, he believes the truth will exonerate you. He lacks confidence in local law enforcement, and I don't blame him."

"He asked you to investigate this yourself?" she asked. "How will you do that?"

"Discreetly." Leaning back, he propped one long leg on a chair. "I've started going through Lowell's papers and talking to people, trying to determine his state of mind and why he would attack you. But this business with the knife makes me wonder."

"Wonder what?" she asked.

"Wonder if I'm taking the wrong tack." His air of concentration deepened. "The assumption has been that you killed Lowell, and the question is what he did to provoke it. Whether he forced your hand, and if so, why?"

"But now?" His answer mattered more than she could say. More, perhaps, than she could bring herself to admit.

"If you were calculating and devious, you might've gone out today and found a duplicate knife." Dirk was assessing the possibilities as if she weren't there. Joni supposed she should be offended, but instead she welcomed his objectivity. "Considering that you just got out of the hospital, that seems unlikely unless you have an accomplice or you bought the knife in advance. In either case, you would have planned a better alibi."

"So, by default, you think somebody else did it?" she asked with a touch of irony.

"Did they?" Cobalt eyes fixed on her. "You ought to know, Joni." He reminded her of a detective holding himself apart from the scene. Yet she had the feeling he was leaning toward her side.

"The murder weapon wasn't my knife." Her head still felt woolly, but at least it had stopped spinning. "I didn't take a knife outside, of any shape or size. Dirk, I didn't even know anyone was out there. I went out to the patio to put Jeff's bike in the garage."

"Why didn't you tell that to the police?" he asked. "Reading the report, I got the impression you went outside to confront Lowell."

"I said I went outside and found Lowell there." Details of the interview eluded her. "At least, I think that's what I said. I was so dazed, I'm not sure how I phrased it."

"So you wouldn't have had any reason to take a knife." His jaw worked. "Except that you *were* being stalked."

"By Lowell," she said. "I think."

"You're not sure about that, either?"

"I never actually saw him or heard his voice on the phone," she admitted. "But it was exactly the same stuff he pulled after I moved out."

"You're sure it was him the first time?"

"He admitted it," she said. "Once we resolved the issues in our divorce, he apologized." Something else occurred to her. "Wednesday night, he did confess that he'd been watching me. He said he saw me come home alone."

"Did he say why or for how long he'd been doing it?" Dirk asked hoarsely.

She shook her head.

"Did my brother ever hit you? In all the time you were married?"

"No." She might have felt intimidated by Lowell's world and in awe of her powerful husband, but she wouldn't have tolerated physical abuse.

Dirk was absorbed in his speculation. "So what we have is someone harassing you, and my brother watching the house, then coming forward to talk to you. You smack your head into the hummingbird feeder and wake up holding a knife. In the meantime, someone has stabbed Lowell to death.''

"Unless I've blocked something out, which is what the police seem to believe.''

"That's what I assumed, too, until now," Dirk said. "Think hard, Joni. Does anyone have a grudge against you or Lowell?''

"Not that I know of. Except Kim, maybe.''

"Any man who's shown you undue attention? What about your boss?''

"Basil's always been kind of strange," she admitted. "But I don't think he's dangerous.''

"How long have you worked for him?''

"A year and three months, roughly. I got a job fairly soon after the divorce.'' Her system must have absorbed energy from lunch because Joni felt stronger now. "He's never asked me out, but he's never come over here before, either.''

Dirk took a small notebook from his pocket and jotted in it. "Any other men?''

She thought of Charlie. "Jeff's soccer coach brought me flowers at the hospital, but I didn't get a chance to talk to him. He's never behaved in a threatening way. I hardly know him.''

"What about women?" he asked. "A rival at work? Or anywhere else?''

"Well, Mrs. Wright never seemed to care for me very much." That was the Petersons' longtime housekeeper. "I don't think I lived up to her notion of the right kind of woman for Lowell.''

"She doted on my brother," Dirk said. "She certainly wouldn't have killed him.''

"So there we are," Joni said. "Back to me with an unidentified knife in my hand."

Dirk put the notebook away. "And the possibility of a killer on the loose."

"But if someone wanted me dead, he—or she—had every opportunity to kill me that night," she noted.

"Maybe he didn't want you dead. Maybe he wants you for himself."

The shivering came from deep inside. Being stalked by Lowell had seemed annoying but only a little scary. The possibility that there might be some madman who believed he could possess Joni aroused a deep and chilling dread.

"You're cold." Dirk leaned toward her protectively.

"No. I'm scared." But she wouldn't let herself panic. She needed to understand the killer so she could figure out who he might be. "If he…wants me, why try to frame me for murder?"

Dirk considered for a moment. "From the profiles I've read of stalkers, a man like that might be trying to punish you. It's all part of his need to take control of your life. Herb said you and Lowell were getting friendly again. That could've set him off."

"But if I were in prison, he couldn't have me."

"Maybe he doesn't think that clearly. Or he might've assumed you'd get off on a plea of self-defense."

The possibility of a psychopathic stalker was almost worse than the fear that she'd stabbed Lowell and blocked it out. "This is so bizarre."

"I could be wrong. There might not be such a man at all." Dirk's tone was noncommittal. "Just to be on the safe side—do you have a security system?"

She shook her head.

"It didn't occur to you that installing one might be a good idea?" His dark eyebrows arched questioningly.

"I didn't believe Lowell would hurt me." In retrospect, Joni wished that she had paid more attention to her ex-husband's protestations of innocence. After talking to Dirk, she was almost certain now that whoever had made those phone calls and committed the vandalism, it hadn't been Lowell but someone else. Someone deadly.

"I don't suppose you keep a gun in the house?"

"Not with an eight-year-old running around. I'd rather something happened to me because I didn't have a gun than have my son get hurt because I did," she asserted.

Dirk's expression softened. "You have that mothering instinct full force, don't you?"

"Of course." She refrained from wondering aloud how he could have so little in the way of fatherly instincts. Men were different from women that way, she supposed. Maybe he realized that a globe-trotter was in no position to raise a child. Or perhaps he'd distanced himself so completely that he didn't think of Jeff as his son.

"Where are your Yellow Pages?"

She blinked at the sudden request. "In the drawer under the phone."

"You're going to get a security system, today if possible." He stood and strode toward the phone. "I'll pay for it."

"Thanks. I'd be grateful." Until now, a household alarm system had sounded like more nuisance than it was worth and the cost would have strained her budget. But she could see that she needed one.

Dirk spent the next twenty minutes on the phone, trying to find a company that would promise immediate installation. Finally, he yielded to the inevitable and made an appointment.

"It's a good system," he said after hanging up. "They'll wire all the windows as well as the doors. Unfortunately, we can't get it installed until Wednesday."

"That sounds so far off."

"It's the soonest anyone could come. I'll sleep here until then." He wasn't asking; he was telling.

"Sleep here?" Joni stared at Dirk as he paced to the window to look out. He had a well-developed build, a bit more compact than Lowell's, and a cocky way of holding himself. This strange, alluring man intended to live in her house for the next five days? "I don't think so."

"What are you worried about—gossip?" he challenged. "As if people weren't already running off at the mouth? Besides, I'm your brother-in-law."

"Ex-brother-in-law."

"Joni," he said, "there's no way I'm leaving you here unguarded."

"Mom?" Jeff wandered through the kitchen doorway. "What are you guys talking about?"

"Your uncle wants to move in for a few days," she said.

"To watch over you." Dirk gave the boy a smile. "If you don't mind."

His little face lit up. "Really? Would you? That would be nice, wouldn't it, Mom?"

Joni's spirits sank. She didn't want her son becoming too attached to Dirk and complicating an already difficult situation. "I don't think it's a good idea."

"Please." Where had that worried frown come from? Jeff seemed to have grown suddenly older. "Dad died right outside. Uncle Dirk knows how to protect us, don't you?''

"I won't let anything happen to either of you." The man set one hand on his son's shoulder. For the first time, Joni noticed that they had matching indentations in their left cheeks.

"I'll sleep better if he's here," Jeff pleaded.

Joni swallowed her objections. Dirk's reassuring presence would help her son through these next few days as he absorbed the fact that he would never see his daddy again. It might help her, too.

"All right," she conceded. "He can stay until we get our security system installed."

"Thanks, Mom," Jeff said, and then, no doubt parroting a phrase he'd heard on television, added, "You won't regret this."

Dirk chuckled. "I certainly hope not."

Joni hoped not, too.

Chapter Six

Both Jeff and Joni retired to bed early. With the house quiet, Dirk went into the kitchen and cleaned up the remains of their fast-food dinner.

Detective MacDougall had come by earlier to collect the knife and interview Joni about it. Dirk couldn't tell from his reaction whether he believed her story, and Joni seemed too exhausted to care.

After grilling her, the man had spent several hours examining the contents of kitchen drawers, the dishwasher and refrigerator, then prowling the patio. Finally, he'd removed the yellow tape and departed with the knife.

In the den, Dirk went to work hanging his clothes in the closet and tucking his underwear into the only drawer in an end table. Cramped quarters, but he'd certainly stayed in worse.

When he'd stopped by the Peterson estate that afternoon to retrieve his belongings, Mrs. Wright had frowned in disapproval at learning that he was moving to Joni's house. After working for his family for twenty years, she was taking Lowell's death hard.

She'd softened after Dirk pointed out that he was staying there for Jeff's sake. But was he really? he wondered as he opened the couch into a bed.

Joni had asked his advice about the knife, but beyond that, she didn't seem to think she needed help. He had a feeling she wasn't used to leaning on anyone.

Damn it, he wanted her to lean on him. Or at least to spend more time with him. He wanted a chance to discover the side of herself that she hid from the world.

Those brown-specked green eyes had a way of confronting him boldly, then flicking shyly away, that made him itch to find out what she was thinking. To touch her skin and feel the silkiness of her hair and surprise her in a hundred subtle ways.

He wondered how Joni would react if he took her in his arms. Whether her mouth would yield beneath his and her body come alive. Whether her hands would grip his shoulders as he eased open the buttons on her blouse...

Great idea, Dirk told himself harshly. If he made love to Joni, then what?

He hated staying in one place for long and backed off at the first sign of anyone trying to rein him in. That was how life had shaped him, and it was too late to change his character now.

During his last year in security work, he'd become involved with a bodyguard named Elena. A beautiful woman with white-blond hair and a crackling sense of humor, she had a black belt in karate but was growing tired of constant travel and danger.

By that time, Dirk was considering leaving the security firm to start his own business. When an entrepreneur for whom he'd consulted offered him a chance to join a new venture, Dirk decided to invest his savings and go for it.

Elena announced she was ready for marriage and children. Dirk wanted those things, too, someday. But, excited about his new challenge, he asked her to give him more time.

His new firm had brokered computer services in a country carved from the former Soviet Union. Dirk worked day and night, setting up a system that matched local companies with experts from around the world. His consultants could do anything from putting together a firm's hardware system to custom-designing its software.

Once the company was running smoothly, Dirk sold his share for a large sum. He'd identified another business opportunity, this one in central Africa, and proposed it to a group of venture capitalists. That led to establishing his own consulting company.

For the first time in his life, he felt in charge and powerful. Like someone his father would have respected.

Tired of waiting, Elena took on another assignment in South America. The man she was protecting turned out to be the target of drug dealers. He died in an ambush of machine-gun fire. So did she.

Remembering the day he'd received the news still felt like a punch in the gut. Dirk had loved Elena, and he'd failed her.

Maybe he hadn't been honest enough, with her or with himself. Maybe he wasn't cut out to be anyone's husband.

In the five years since then, he'd always seemed to need another mountain to climb. Just thinking about some of the projects he was juggling made the adrenaline start to pump.

Joni didn't strike him as the type to want a short-term affair, and Dirk didn't intend to hang around Viento del Mar for long. The best thing he could do would be to watch over her, strictly as a friend, until she recovered her health.

That, and find out what had happened to his brother.

As he went into the hall bathroom to stow his shaving kit, Dirk heard steady breathing from Jeff's bedroom. Joni's door was closed, and he guessed she would be asleep by now, too.

His watch showed five past eight. It was at about this hour two nights ago that his brother had been slain.

If he walked through the scenario from Lowell's perspective, trying to view it with his brother's eyes, he might gain a better understanding of what had happened. Experience had taught him that even the smallest details could change the big picture.

First, Dirk decided, he had to set the scene as it had been that night. Remembering the description from the police report, he switched on the rear porch light. Leaving the kitchen and den illuminated, he donned a windbreaker, picked up a flashlight and went outside.

Lowell's car had been found around the block, parked out of sight. No one recalled seeing any other strange cars in the neighborhood, although he wasn't sure the police had talked to all possible witnesses.

MacDougall had speculated that Lowell must have watched the property from behind, on the slope, although the rain had destroyed any evidence of where he'd waited. Lowell had been wearing a thin suit, though, so he hadn't come prepared for a lengthy stakeout.

Dirk decided to start in front. His brother must have arrived from that direction at some point. Besides, for security reasons, it was important to get a sense of how the area looked after dark.

He descended the sloping driveway, past his rented

sedan. Down the street, a car turned into a driveway, its headlights cutting a swath through the darkness before shutting off. Somewhere a dog barked, once, twice, and then stopped.

Darkness fell, deep and layered. There was no street-level illumination, and clouds blocked the moon. Even through the windbreaker, Dirk could feel the October chill.

Standing in front of the house, he scanned the neighborhood. All the structures were one story; from seeing them in daylight, he recalled that they were stucco with wood trim, designed to blend with the environment.

On Joni's side, the houses sat against the perimeter of the development, with only woodlands beyond. On the opposite side of the street, the residences were half-hidden on rolling lots.

Just beyond Joni's place lay a cul-de-sac. Because of the curvature and an intervening stand of trees, the end house was some distance away and at an angle that made it unlikely the occupants could see much of her front yard, let alone the back.

Turning, Dirk scrutinized Joni's house. Light glimmered from the living room, while the thin front curtain allowed a glimpse inside. All he could see, though, was a framed print on the wall. Not enough to satisfy anyone intent on observing her. A watcher would have to choose a position behind the house all right.

According to Dirk's research, the woods stretched for miles, crossed by a few hiking trails. Only someone who knew the area could have come that way by night.

Lowell had never been the outdoor type. In addition, although he could be impulsive, his temper usually subsided with time. He might not be quick to forgive, but he wasn't the type to calculate a slow-burning revenge, either.

Yet he admitted he was watching Joni. Why?

Hands jammed into his pockets, Dirk trudged up the driveway. He didn't want to believe that his brother had threatened her, any more than he wanted to accept that she had killed him. So far, however, nothing but the existence of a second knife indicated a third party might have been involved. Until he found more evidence, he must not let wishful thinking affect his judgment.

Joni reminded Dirk a lot of himself in his younger days, when he'd had to weather his father's faultfinding and Lowell's frequent digs. He, too, had built up a cautious exterior and learned to hold his feelings inside. Most of the time anyway. That didn't mean she was like him in other ways. Even Herb had some doubts about her, or why would he have pressed Dirk to begin this investigation?

At the top of the driveway, he followed a concrete walkway behind the garage. Stopping short of the diffused glow from the porch light, Dirk surveyed the patio. Even in moonlight, it was full of shadows, and the sky had been overcast on Wednesday. Joni had said she didn't realize anyone was there until the last minute, and he could believe it.

Dirk turned his attention to the slope, or what little he could see of it. It would be almost impossible to descend in the dark without making a racket. Besides, Joni had said Lowell came from this side, near the garage.

There was nowhere to hide, this close to the house. Swinging around, Dirk headed for the short drop that divided Joni's yard from the neighbor's. As he neared the divide, the leaves of a thick shrub grazed his face. He pushed them aside, then realized as they rustled and swayed that what he'd assumed was a bush was instead a long branch.

With his flashlight, Dirk traced it backward. The branch and several others arced outward from a tree located a short ways uphill, on the property line.

What had appeared to be a dense plant was instead a canopy formed by overgrown branches. In the space he had assumed would be filled by a thick trunk, there was room for a man to hide.

This cover stood no more than a dozen long strides from Joni's back door. From here, through the rear windows, Dirk could have seen anyone standing at the sink or sitting at the kitchen table. He could also see the street and any cars that might come up the driveway.

He shone his flashlight inside the blind, at the ground. When something glistened, Dirk knelt to check it out.

Just a piece of quartz, he found to his disappointment. Then, still crouching, he spotted the heel print.

It was a faint impression, but deep enough for him to see the kind of tread that came from an athletic shoe. The night Lowell died, according to the police report, he'd been wearing smooth-soled Italian leather.

Dirk trained the flashlight closer. The shallow print showed no sign of rain damage. It must have been made since Wednesday night.

His arms prickled. Someone had been watching the house yesterday or today. Watching Joni. And Jeff. And him.

Detective MacDougall must have gone home for the night by now. He wouldn't appreciate being rousted at this hour for anything less than an emergency, and this didn't qualify. But Dirk vowed to call the man first thing in the morning.

He wondered if Lowell had discovered the blind, or

if he'd waited for Joni, oblivious, only a few feet from a hidden observer. It was an unnerving possibility.

To complete the survey, Dirk retraced his steps toward the patio. The dusty light globe glared into his eyes, blocking his vision as it would have done to Lowell in his final moments of life. His brother could have made out Joni's figure on the patio, but he couldn't have seen much beyond that. The slope to his left and the lawn and trees beyond the patio were blotted out.

And, of course, he wouldn't have seen someone approaching from behind. From the leafy hideout.

In the woods, a coyote howled, its wail bouncing and echoing. The sound made Dirk jump. Annoyed at himself, he crossed the patio, skirting the heavy glass table. It took several seconds before his night vision returned.

From a reverse angle, he surveyed the scene. The patio. The slope. The trees above, black against a charcoal sky.

In the woods, he spotted a pinprick of light.

Dirk stared at it in confusion. For a moment, he thought it might be a safety light, but why only one? Besides, it wasn't large enough to provide security.

Then it moved. Gripping the flashlight, he aimed it up the slope, but its beam wasn't strong enough to penetrate that far. The light vanished. Did the intruder realize he'd been noticed?

Instinct urged Dirk to give chase, but the other person had a head start and knew the terrain. A newcomer would likely reap nothing more than a twisted ankle. Worse, he would leave Joni unguarded.

There was no proof, of course, that this person had any connection to Wednesday's tragedy. Anyone who lived in the area might be taking a walk.

But only a fool ignored patterns, and one was definitely taking shape here. The second knife. The footprint inside a hiding place. The light on the hill.

The odds had shifted. It seemed less and less likely that Joni had been the one who wielded the murder weapon. Or that his brother had been her stalker. More likely, Lowell had appointed himself as lookout to nab the prowler in the act. A prowler who was still free, his existence not even suspected by the police.

To keep his promise to Herb, Dirk would have to expand his scope. Instead of a narrow probe into Lowell's state of mind, he was now looking for a killer who might be anyone.

JONI AWOKE SHORTLY AFTER nine o'clock on Saturday morning. She couldn't remember the last time she'd slept this late.

From the den came the chatter of a cartoon show. Outside, a car turned into the driveway. Dragging herself to the window, she spotted a light brown sedan with Detective MacDougall at the wheel. What was he doing here?

Moving stiffly, she pulled on some clothes, brushed her teeth and ran a comb through her hair. After downing some aspirin, she went into the den.

"Uncle Dirk's in the backyard," Jeff announced from where he sat watching TV.

"Is the police officer with him?"

"I guess so." He showed no further interest. Normally, her son was underfoot when anything happened, peppering the grown-ups with questions.

"Jeff?" she said. "Do you feel all right?"

"I just don't want to go outside." His hunched shoulders revealed more about his anxiety than any words could have.

Joni gave her son a hug. He'd lost his father and, on top of that, had to deal with the fact that the death had occurred under their noses. She wished she could make the pain go away, but children, like adults, needed time to grieve.

"I love you," she said. "Everything's under control, honey. Okay?"

"Okay." He returned his gaze to the screen, obviously uncomfortable with talking about his feelings.

In any case, Joni needed to find out what the detective was doing. She wouldn't be much good to her son if she went to prison. Between her house and the neighbor's, she found Dirk holding up a heavy branch for the detective, who was inspecting the ground. Behind MacDougall stood Celia, watching with lively interest.

"What's going on?" Joni asked.

Three faces turned toward her. "Your brother-in-law has discovered a possible hideout for our stalker," MacDougall said. "Only problem is, there's no evidence anyone's used it."

"There was a heel print here last night." Dirk brushed a lock of dark hair from his forehead. "Someone's erased it. And I saw a light moving in the woods."

"You came out here last night?" she asked.

"I figured I might learn something if I retraced Lowell's steps," he said. "Apparently, I was right."

Celia hugged herself. Although she was neatly dressed in an embroidered blouse over black pants, her tangled hair indicated she'd dressed quickly. "You saw someone on hill? What time?"

"About eight-thirty," Dirk said. "He must have seen me discover the blind."

Joni's hands went cold. If it were a casual hiker, he

wouldn't have erased the footprint. There really *was* someone watching her house.

The detective looked up from making notes. "This does put a different slant on things, although it's too bad we don't have the print. You say it was some kind of athletic shoe?"

"I couldn't be sure which brand, but it was that type of tread."

"Lowell never wore his Nike shoes outside the health club." Joni barely managed to keep her voice steady.

"I don't believe my brother could have left that print. It showed no rain damage." Dirk's concerned gaze met hers.

He'd shaved this morning and put on a V-necked navy sweater over a crisp tan shirt and pressed jeans. It seemed unfair that anyone could look so well put together this early on a Saturday, she reflected irrelevantly.

"Have you seen any prowlers, ma'am?" the detective asked Celia.

"No, but I keep my blinds drawn after dark," she said. "Especially when my husband's away." He had departed the previous week for a monthlong business trip to Taiwan and Singapore.

MacDougall checked the area. Then, accompanied by Dirk, he stomped up the slope to the edge of the woods. Leaving Celia to trail them, Joni went inside.

Judging by the crumb-covered plates in the kitchen sink, her son and Dirk had already fixed toast for breakfast. Since Jeff was afraid of burning himself, Dirk must have toasted the bread for both of them.

A mother excelled at detective work when it came to figuring out household behavior, she thought wryly. Too bad she couldn't do the same for a murder.

As she fixed herself a bowl of cereal, Joni reviewed

what Dirk had discovered. The footprint and the way it had been wiped clean, together with the knife, dispelled any lingering doubts. She knew with absolute certainty that she hadn't stabbed Lowell.

She was glad Jeff wouldn't have to grow up with the knowledge that his mother had killed his father, even in self-defense. And whatever Lowell might have done in the past, it repelled her to think of wreaking such violence on a man she'd once loved.

But now, Joni thought grimly, she had to deal with the frightening prospect that remained. A murderer had been on her property last night.

She was grateful that her brother-in-law had security training. And that he cared enough about the truth to keep searching for it when the police had been ready to accept her guilt at face value. She wondered whether his support had anything to do with his being Jeff's biological father. In truth, his motivation no longer mattered. She was just glad he was here.

"Mom?" Jeff wandered in, holding a stuffed dragon named Yoshi. To her knowledge, he hadn't carried it out of his bedroom in months, but now, apparently, he needed the reassurance. "Don't I have a soccer game?"

"Oh, my gosh!" She jumped up. "I'm not supposed to bring the snacks today, am I?"

"You brought granola bars last week," her son reminded her.

She sighed. "Oh, right. Where would I be without your memory?"

"Panicking," Jeff said tartly, and went off to change clothes.

The prospect of attending the game lifted Joni's spirits. She needed something normal to hang on to, and what could be more normal than kids' soccer?

She was sitting on the edge of the opened couch in the den, lacing her tennis shoes, when Dirk came in. Outside, the detective's car rattled away.

"Find anything?" she asked.

His mouth twisted. "Nothing. No pun intended. By the way, I trimmed back the branches as far as I could with the tools from your garage. I don't think anyone will be hiding there for a while."

"Thanks," Joni said. "Dirk, your help means more than I can say."

"That's why I'm here." The flimsy sofa bed sank as he sat beside her. "It's why you have to put up with my dishes in the sink and my shaving kit in the bathroom."

"I don't mind. Not at all." It must be the light-headedness from her injury, Joni thought, that made her so aware that she was sitting next to an incredibly desirable man. His spicy scent pervaded the sheets and surrounded her like a cocoon. She ached to curve against his broad chest and feel the strength of those muscular shoulders. To cup his well-shaped head in her hands.

A bed. A man. What would it feel like to lie here with him?

She didn't intend to find out. Life was too complicated already.

Down the hall, she could hear Jeff clomping about in his bedroom. The boy could make more noise fishing his shin guards and spiked shoes out of the closet than Joni could make dropping an entire stack of pots and pans. Well, almost.

"Something going on?" Dirk raised an eyebrow.

"Soccer game," she said.

"You're into that?" An indentation flashed in his cheek as he smiled. "Do you realize that soccer moms have become legendary?"

"I'm not much of a soccer mom," Joni confessed as she retied one shoe. "I hid in the back when they asked for someone to make the team banner."

"Didn't they catch you?" he teased.

"No, but Jeff's best friend's mother volunteered." Joni sighed. "I had to spend a whole Sunday afternoon helping her cut out pieces of felt and glue them together. It looks pretty good, no thanks to me. Kathryn's the talented one."

"Where do they hold these games?" he asked.

"It depends on who else needs the fields. Today we're playing at the high school." Joni stood, trying to convince herself that she didn't feel the other shoelace working its way loose.

"This should be interesting." Dirk uncoiled from the low bed.

"You're coming?"

"Whoever's been watching you is most likely an acquaintance," he said. "I need to get to know your friends."

Jeff trudged in, wearing shorts and a jersey in the team colors of black and silver. "Are you coming, Uncle Dirk?"

"I wouldn't miss it."

The boy straightened as if an invisible burden had been lifted. "Great!"

The two of them walked ahead of Joni through the house. Their sturdy gaits had the same boyish swing, she noticed with a pang.

They took Dirk's car. It was a pleasure, Joni discovered, to get away from the house.

As sunshine flooded through the windshield, an oldies song bounced from the radio. In the back seat, Jeff danced in place. Amused, Dirk kept glancing at the boy in the rearview mirror.

Being together, the three of them, felt like the old days when she'd been part of a two-parent family, Joni mused. She hadn't realized how much she'd missed that sense of completion.

But a deep uneasiness refused to let her enjoy the good mood for long. As they turned left from Canyon Acres onto San Bernardo Road, Joni remembered what Dirk had said earlier. *Whoever's been watching you is most likely an acquaintance.*

In the bustle of getting out the door, she hadn't given his assertion much thought. Now it struck her with painful clarity.

The stalker might be someone they would see at the game. The coach or his assistant. One of the parents. A soccer-league official.

Until this case was resolved, she couldn't trust anyone. She had to stay on the alert, even among friends. Or perhaps, as Dirk had indicated, especially among friends.

Chapter Seven

Cars filled much of the high school parking lot. It was a quarter to eleven, Joni saw from her watch, and pre-game practice had started half an hour ago. Jeff had missed that, but at least he'd attended practice last Wednesday. And he was here for the game.

"I didn't realize soccer was so popular." Dirk angled his rental car between a van and a station wagon. "There are quite a few cars here."

"There are two teams with about a dozen kids on each, so it does get crowded." A synchronized cheer drifted from the nearby gymnasium. "Also, it sounds like the cheerleaders are practicing today, too."

"This whole scene reminds me of a sixties TV show about middle America." Dirk cut off the engine. "It's another lifetime, if not another world."

"You grew up here," Joni pointed out. "It shouldn't seem *that* strange."

"After watching *Melrose Place* in Nairobi and *The Brady Bunch* in Bombay, dubbed into the local languages, it's hard to view America the same way," he said.

"There's Coach!" Grabbing his soccer ball, Jeff

waved to Charlie, who was shading his eyes on the playing field. The coach waved back.

"Bobby's here." Joni pointed to the Owenses' white minivan, distinguished by the black and silver racing stripes Kathryn had painted along the side.

"Bobby, I take it, is a good friend?" Dirk asked his nephew.

"The best!" Jeff loped ahead of them across the blacktop, and on the field his friends cheered his approach.

"We should have been here early for practice," Joni admitted as she walked beside Dirk. Her head and ribs ached dully. "I hope that, under the circumstances, the coach will understand."

"Whether he understands isn't important," he said. "Joni, I know these are familiar surroundings, but this situation isn't normal. You can't afford to let your guard down. You have to imagine we're in a foreign country where we don't know whom to trust."

Was that possible? she wondered as they passed a group of three team mothers, one with a baby in a stroller, the others shepherding toddlers. Exchanging startled glances, the women turned away without greeting Joni. They'd always acted friendly before, but until now, she reflected, she hadn't been suspected of killing anyone.

"I guess I might as well be in a foreign country," she agreed sadly.

On the playing field, Jeff joined the other boys milling around. As his assistant herded them into line, the coach turned to stare at Joni.

She waved. "Thanks for the flowers!"

He nodded, but his half smile vanished as he turned

his attention to Dirk. Was she imagining it, or was that a look of hostility?

Tapping her companion's arm, she asked, "Do you know him?"

Dirk glanced at the coach. "Not that I recall. Did he grow up around here?"

Now that she thought about it, Joni recalled hearing that Charlie had moved to town a couple of years ago. "I guess not. He seems to have taken a dislike to you, though."

The man on the field turned abruptly away. "Temper, temper," Dirk murmured. "You said he's been paying attention to you? I need to have a talk with that guy."

To their left, a silver-and-black banner displayed a soccer ball and the slogan, "Win, Raiders!" Across the field, a blue-and-white banner proclaimed, "Sting 'Em, Hornets!" In both sets of bleachers, parents were spreading out their blankets.

"Friendly rivalry?" Dirk asked.

"Most of the time," she said. "Some of the parents get carried away. Did you ever play when you were a kid?"

"One season of Little League," he said. "That was the popular sport back then."

"Lowell had a couple of trophies," she recalled. "He encouraged Jeff to go out for soccer."

"My brother was a star." Dirk spoke without rancor. "Maybe I could've been, maybe not. What I couldn't take was my father standing on the sidelines screaming at me whenever I made a mistake. How well did you know Dad anyway?"

Donald Peterson had been the hard-driving head of Peterson Printing when Joni went to work there. To her, he'd remained a distant, intimidating figure until his death from a heart attack two years after her marriage.

"Not well," she admitted. "I was grateful he didn't object to Lowell's marrying me."

"Knowing my father, he saw you as suitable material to carry on the line," Dirk said. "An obedient wife who wouldn't put her career or her social life ahead of having children."

"I never considered it that way." It hadn't occurred to Joni that a lack of accomplishments might be viewed as an advantage. "Oh, there are the Owenses! Let me introduce you."

From halfway up the bleachers, Bobby's parents greeted her warmly, a welcome contrast to the other parents' reactions. When she introduced Dirk and explained that he was staying with her, Kathryn's immediate response was "I'll bet that makes Jeff feel safer!"

"Jeff isn't the only one," Joni confessed as they took seats on her friends' blanket.

"But surely there's no danger to you now." Worry creased Fred's round, pinkish face. Of average height, he played basketball several times a week to battle his tendency to put on weight. "I don't mean to be insensitive, but with Lowell gone—"

"We're not certain my brother was the one stalking her," Dirk said.

"Really?" Kathryn glanced in alarm from him to Joni. "You mean there's been more harassment?"

"No." Joni didn't feel like going into detail about the footprint in the blind and the knife in the dishwasher. "There are a few pieces that don't fit."

"If you'll excuse me, I'm going to try to talk to the coach before the game starts." With quick, sure footing, Dirk swung down.

"Someone should warn him that Charlie's never in a mood to chat at game time," Kathryn sighed, finger combing her short brown hair.

"What does he want to talk to Coach about?" Fred asked.

Joni didn't want to reveal that Dirk was conducting his own investigation; if word ever reached MacDougall, he'd be furious. "He's taking an interest in my son. I don't see how it can hurt."

"Perhaps not," Kathryn said. "As long as he's realistic. He might mean well, but no one can replace Jeff's father."

"He isn't too much like his brother, is he?" Fred added in concern. "I mean, he's living in your house, Joni. What if he gives you a hard time?"

"It's only until I can get an alarm system installed," she said. "Besides, believe me, I would never allow a man to treat me the way Lowell did ever again."

Below, Charlie brushed off Dirk's attempts to talk and marched onto the field. Dirk remained in place, watching the coach and the players.

Color and movement in the parking lot distracted her. Joni noticed a group of cheerleaders in orange-and-purple costumes scattering to their parents' cars. A few, probably sisters of soccer players, headed toward the bleachers.

Among them prowled a tall woman with a sculpted face and long, dark hair as silky as a model's. She was, as everyone knew, the volunteer cheerleading coach. She was also the woman who had broken up Joni's marriage.

Kim DeLong, dressed in a black silk blouse and matching leggings, strode toward one of her society friends in the opposing bleachers. Halfway there, she paused to stretch like a cat, the movements displaying her curves to maximum effect.

Men gawked. Some of the women frowned, but Joni knew that none of them would dare reproach the woman. From her father, Kim had inherited a large share of the town's commercial real estate and a leading position in society, and she was known to be vindictive.

Kim and Lowell had been a golden couple all through high school. Because they were five years older than Joni, she hadn't known them then, but she'd seen their pictures in the newspaper. They'd been shimmeringly beautiful and mind-numbingly rich.

During college, the two had dated for a while. Then an older man, a banker from San Francisco, won Kim away. She'd married him after graduation, reportedly breaking Lowell's heart.

He'd quickly recovered and married Joni. When Kim divorced her husband half a dozen years later and moved back to Viento del Mar, Lowell hadn't shown any interest.

Only after Kim called to brag about her conquest did Joni learn that, according to gossip, the raven-haired woman had set her sights on Lowell from the day she returned. Maybe, the busybodies said, he'd been dissatisfied with his wife; he had certainly criticized her enough. Joni suspected he'd also been flattered by Kim's pursuit and too self-centered to consider what it meant to break his marriage vows.

On the field, the game began, but she found it hard to concentrate. Seeing Kim brought back unpleasant memories and in addition her over-the-counter pain medication was wearing off. Her ribs throbbed and she had to grip the seat more than once until her head stopped spinning.

At first, Jeff played carelessly, without his usual spirit. After a while, though, he got caught up in the game and even scored a goal. From her spot, she could see Dirk studying the crowd and knew he must have noted Kim's arrival. But he spent most of his time calling out encouragement to Jeff.

Kathryn had implied that Dirk might be trying to take Lowell's place. Neither the Owenses nor anyone else, even Herb, knew the truth about Jeff's parentage, but Joni supposed her friend's speculation might not be entirely wrong. Even though she no longer believed Dirk would seek custody, he seemed to be drawing closer to his son. If he did want an ongoing relationship, it would mean spending more time in Viento del Mar.

With a start, she realized that the prospect pleased her. She felt more comfortable talking with Dirk than she ever had with Lowell, and his physical nearness brought a new awareness of her own femininity.

Her husband had been classically handsome but remote. Dirk, on the other hand, made her breath come faster every time she glanced at him. In a visceral, intensely personal way, she wanted him.

Disturbed, Joni stared down at the man pacing beside the field. The last thing she needed was to let herself become vulnerable to him. Losing Lowell had hurt badly; if she ever allowed herself to fall in love with Dirk, how could she bear to give him up? This time she knew in advance that she couldn't keep him. Only a fool would set herself up for that kind of loss.

A murmur from the bleachers roused Joni into the present. Coach Charlie, who had bent to pick up a soccer ball, had split his pants up the back seam. Judging by his red face, he didn't find the incident funny.

"Those uniforms aren't made very well," Kathryn said. "How embarrassing."

"The problem is, he's put on weight," Fred observed. "Don't blame the pants."

After muttering a few words to his assistant, the coach marched toward the parking lot. Joni hoped he had some extra pants in his car; the game was a close one, and the kids needed his guidance. Sure enough, by the end of halftime, he returned in a fresh pair of sweats. For the rest of the game, however, Charlie let his assistant do the strenuous bending.

"I can't understand why the man's let himself go," Fred commented. "He ought to be in shape. After all, he teaches exercise classes."

"Is that what he does for a living?" Charlie was one of the soccer league's best volunteer coaches, but Joni had no idea of his regular occupation.

"No," Kathryn said. "He works for a plumbing service— Oh, I can't look!" She covered her eyes as an opposing player stole the ball from Bobby right in front of the Hornets' goal.

Instantly, Jeff darted in and stole it back. With a fierce kick, he knocked the black-and-white orb past the goalie and into the net.

The crowd cheered. Below, Dirk raised both fists in triumph.

"Don't worry, dear." Fred patted his wife's hand. "Joni's son saved the day."

The game ended a few minutes later, 4-to-3 in favor of the black and silver. The Raiders lined up to call "Good game!" to their rivals. The Hornets returned the sentiment but without enthusiasm.

Teaching sportsmanship was one of the goals of the soccer league, but Joni wasn't sure the lessons stuck very well. Especially not with some parents. Right now, in the stands opposite, a father was chewing out a tearful little boy who had missed an easy goal. She winced at a mental image of Donald Peterson yelling at a childish Dirk.

Lowell had tried the same tactic once, but the boy had indignantly ordered his father to stop being so mean. After a moment's stunned silence, Lowell had apologized. She wondered whether it was an innate character trait or the result of being an only child that had given Jeff the nerve to fight back.

Dirk, on the other hand, had withdrawn from the sport. He didn't shrink from confrontations anymore, though, she decided, watching him pace across the field toward Kim DeLong.

She supposed he wanted to question the woman about Lowell. It made sense, but that knowledge didn't stop a twinge of jealousy at seeing Kim straighten her shoulders and greet him with the calculated smile she reserved for good-looking men.

People crossed the stands in front of Joni, blocking her view. "Need help?" Fred, shifting a cooler to his other hand, offered an arm.

"I sure do." Shakily, she held on to him as they followed Kathryn down from the bleachers. "You're a lifesaver."

"That's what friends are for." At ground level, he bent to give Bobby a hug. "Terrific game!"

"Yeah!" The boy beamed. "Hey, Mrs. Peterson, can Jeff come home with us?"

"Please?" her son chimed from beside his friend. "We want to work on our Halloween costumes."

"Oh, that's right, it's next Thursday." Joni hadn't even considered what her son would wear.

"We both want to be Wishbone." The boys loved the spotted dog who acted out canine versions of classic stories on PBS.

"Both of you as one dog?" Fred raised an eyebrow teasingly.

"In *The Prince and the Pooch,* he's twins," Jeff explained.

Starting to nod her understanding, Joni nearly lost her balance. Kathryn caught her shoulder. "You need to rest, so let us take Jeff for a while. Anyway, I need to measure the boys for their costumes. I've got some old material that might work. Do you want us to drop you at home?"

The dizziness passed. "I'll wait for Dirk."

"We'll bring Jeff by later, then." After making sure Joni could stand unsupported, her friends departed to stow the boys, soccer equipment and other gear into their van.

Maybe she should have accepted their invitation to go home, Joni thought. She knew she'd overextended herself so soon after leaving the hospital. But she wanted to find out what Kim was saying to Dirk. And to see for herself how he reacted to Viento del Mar's resident siren.

By the time she traversed the grass, most of the parents had left. Only a few of Kim's friends lingered nearby, none of them willing to meet Joni's gaze.

Kim's voice grew louder as she spotted the newcomer. "As I said, I don't believe there ever was any harassment. I think she made it up and then lured him there so her kid could get his money."

From Dirk's tone, Joni could tell he was straining for patience. "I wish you would try to remember what Lowell said the last time you talked to him. Whether he'd received any threats or was suspicious of anyone.''

"What's the point?" At close range, the sunlight picked out a few strands of gray in Kim's hair, but she was still a stunning beauty. "The police know who killed him and so does everybody else. The only question is, why haven't they locked her up yet?''

Joni could feel her cheeks flaming, but she stood her ground. "Sometimes what 'everybody' knows is wrong," she said evenly. "If you really cared about Lowell, you'd help his brother find the truth.''

Rage glittered in the woman's eyes. "If *I* cared about him?" she snapped. "I was the great love of his life. Ask anybody in this town. He only married you on the rebound. We may have made a few mistakes, Lowell and I, but we belonged together.''

Joni didn't want to argue the point. "Then I should think you would want to make sure the guilty person gets convicted.''

"The guilty person *will* be convicted!" A pom-pom pin heaved atop Kim's bosom, its orange-and-purple fringe quivering. "He would've come back to me eventually, but you couldn't stand that, could you? You cheap, social-climbing little tramp!''

Her pitch had risen, and Joni realized the ugly words might carry as far as the parking lot. She checked in that direction to make sure Jeff hadn't heard.

The only person visible was Fred, who finished stowing gear in the rear compartment, slammed the hatch and gave Joni a thumbs-up. The gesture of support eased her embarrassment but only slightly. Kim's friends were exchanging knowing glances. It was clear they relished this attack on someone they'd long viewed as an interloper.

"I'd be careful whom I was calling cheap, if I were

you." Dirk's low, furious response brought a shocked stare from Kim. "Do you think my family appreciates your having an affair with my brother and then calling his wife to brag about it? That's not exactly high-class behavior in anybody's book."

Kim's mouth tightened, but she appeared to be weighing her response. Not so much because Dirk had spoken the truth, Joni supposed, as because his family also ranked at the top of the town's social hierarchy.

"You want to make me the bad guy? Suit yourself." Turning, Kim told her friends, "See you later," and headed for the parking lot. The others, subdued, collected their children and departed.

"Thank you." Joni's throat caught as she gazed at Dirk.

He touched her waist, sending darts of pure pleasure streaking through her. "That woman had it coming. I don't excuse my brother's adultery, but she's never shown a moment's remorse for the harm she did you and Jeff. Even Herb despises her although he's too polite to say so."

She tried to keep her tone light. "Gee, I thought you were my personal knight in shining armor, and instead you were just defending the family honor."

A smile flashed across his lean face, but he sobered quickly. "It's the same thing, Joni. You're part of the Peterson family. Herb and I both think of you that way."

The glow of her gallant rescue dimmed. Not that she minded being considered a Peterson, but Joni realized she'd been hoping for a more personal response. She ought to be grateful that she hadn't received one, she reminded herself. She needed to keep her distance.

"Jeff went home with the Owenses," she said. "So I can rest."

"Have you known them long?"

The man didn't trust anyone! "Three years, since the kids started school together," she said.

"I'm glad to see they're sticking by you." He guided her away from the stands. "Let's get you home, shall we?"

The sudden tensing of his body sent a spurt of fear rushing through her. Joni braced for danger until she saw the reason for his reaction.

Red liquid smeared the hood of his blue car, spattering the windshield and dripping onto the bumper. It appeared that someone had tossed a can of paint onto the hood and fled. She saw no scrawled slogans or messages.

The nearby parking slots were empty. With a shake of his head, Dirk bent to check the pavement, possibly for footprints.

"I can't imagine who did this," Joni said. "We've never had vandalism at a game before."

"I doubt this is a random act." He circled the sedan. "If it were, it's likely that paint would've been thrown onto other cars, and someone would undoubtedly have called the police."

"Do you think Kim did it?" Joni asked dubiously. "She was angry, but I have trouble imagining that she carries a bucket of paint in her car."

"The coach was out here for a long time after he ripped his pants," Dirk said. "He didn't look as if he liked me very much, either."

"Could be a lot of people." She sighed.

Pulling a tissue from his pocket, he spit on it and rubbed the paint. The tissue came away streaked with pink. "It's water soluble, which means it might wash off. I'm sure the car rental company would appreciate that."

"Aren't you going to report it?"

Dirk pulled his cellular phone from his pocket. "I doubt it'll do much good, and you need to rest. But I suppose we'd better."

Joni nearly regretted making the suggestion by the time the police got through. Although one of the officers let her sit in his car, it wasn't much more comfortable than the bleachers, and MacDougall spent an interminable amount of time taking samples and looking around the lot.

Worse, he didn't find anything useful. No telltale athletic shoe print, nothing to link the incident to anyone specific.

"We'll have the lab test the substance," the detective said, "but I'd say it's some kids pulling a prank."

Dirk didn't look satisfied, but he held his tongue.

Finally, the police departed and Joni sank wearily into the front seat of the rental. At least the windows remained clear enough for Dirk to drive. As he slid behind the wheel, she said, "By the way, I appreciated how you encouraged Jeff."

"He's a good kid."

In her concern over the paint, she'd almost forgotten the game's exciting climax. "He even scored the winning goal."

"I'm just proud of him for doing his best."

The way Dirk's mouth quirked reminded Joni so sharply of her son that she reached out to cup his cheek. When she pulled her hand away, it retained a lingering impression of firm skin with a hint of masculine roughness. "You remind me so much of him sometimes," she explained.

"Of Lowell?" He backed out of the space.

"No, Jeff."

Dirk pulled into the street, sitting stiffly erect. Finally, almost as if asking a question, he said, "He has our mother's coloring."

Joni supposed she should drop the subject. With Lowell, she'd learned to navigate a conversation as though it were a minefield. Some subjects, such as her own impoverished background and his relationship with his brother, had been guaranteed to put a chill in the air. From Dirk's reticence, she gathered that Jeff's parentage was similar forbidden ground. Well, she was tired of circumspection. They needed to get the subject out in the open.

"Why are you in such denial about it?" she asked.

"About what?"

He was deliberately being obtuse, which confused her. It was uncharacteristic of Dirk. "About Jeff. Being his father, I mean."

He slammed on the brakes. They'd reached a stop sign, but that didn't explain the abruptness.

"What?" As the word exploded from his mouth, amazement transformed his face.

He hadn't known. At the realization, Joni's stomach tightened. How was this possible? What on earth was going on?

And what sort of Pandora's box had she just opened?

Chapter Eight

"You do remember donating sperm, don't you?" Joni's words echoed in Dirk's ears.

He felt as if he'd stepped into an alternate reality. Could Jeff be his son after all? "Yes, but Lowell said it wasn't needed."

Behind them, a car honked. He tapped the gas and turned onto San Bernardo Road.

Joni clasped her hands so tightly the knuckles whitened. "He told you Jeff was his?"

"It isn't true?"

"I can't believe—"

"I had no idea—"

They both stopped. After a moment, Joni said, "There's no question about it. Once the doctors found he was sterile, Lowell never darkened their doors again. I went by myself for the inseminations."

"They couldn't have found some way to use his sperm?"

"He never provided any more," she said. "It was as if he wanted to put the whole thing out of his head."

"Jeff's my son," he said wonderingly.

"It never occurred to me that Lowell would lie to you," she admitted.

Dirk drove in silence as he tried to absorb this startling news. Finally, he said, "Do you think Lowell...that he held it against Jeff?"

Joni picked a loose strip of blush-colored polish from one fingernail. "Not that I could tell. He wasn't the type to change diapers or push a stroller, but I think he loved our son. Since the divorce, he'd made a real effort to spend time with him."

Dirk's mind surged with more questions, many of them difficult to put into words. One took shape at last. "Who else knows?"

"No one," she said. "Donald was already dead, and we saw no reason to tell Herb."

"What about Jeff?"

A slight shake of her head rippled her hair. She'd worn it loose today, in a long blond pageboy that made her look like a teenager. "I do want to tell him eventually, but I have to find the right way and the right time. I don't want to confuse him."

Confuse him? Dirk thought wryly. How about confusing an adult male who was trying, painfully, to absorb an impossible fact?

He had a son. A child. His own offspring.

He'd known this was possible, of course, when he made the donation, but he'd figured a child would belong to him only in the most abstract sense. In real life, any issue would be Lowell's, legally and emotionally.

Now Lowell was gone. And Dirk wasn't merely an uncle anymore. This revelation had changed everything in his universe.

They pulled into Joni's driveway. As he exited the car, Dirk scanned the area for danger and was even more relieved than usual not to see anything amiss. One crisis at a time was plenty.

In the kitchen, Joni heated soup and rolls for lunch. "I guess I dropped a bombshell, huh?" she said. "I assumed you knew."

"A reasonable assumption," he admitted. "What on earth was my brother thinking when he made up such a story?"

"That you would never find out, I suppose." She carried their soup mugs to the table. "If Lowell were alive, you wouldn't have."

"Lies have a way of being found out, don't they?" he said. "I'm glad you want to tell…Jeff the truth." He couldn't say the words "our son." Jeff had been Lowell's son for eight years, and that bond would never, and should never, be entirely broken.

As he ate, Dirk was struck by the casual intimacy of the scene. He was sitting across a kitchen table from the woman who had borne him a child.

From her scattering of freckles to the unaltered boyishness of her body, there was something intrinsically honest about Joni. Wispy bangs fell across her forehead as she curled in the chair, regarding him with mingled sympathy and wariness.

He relished being able to read her moods, at least some of the time. For a man who had learned early to hide his own feelings, her emotional openness came as a relief.

"How would you like to handle this?" he asked.

"Breaking the news to Jeff, you mean?"

"Not exactly." He buttered a roll, paying so little attention that he buttered his index finger, as well. "You know my work is overseas, which puts quite a distance between us. Would you like me to come home for holidays, that sort of thing? We could work out a schedule, something you and Jeff could count on."

"Dirk, I never meant to impose on you." Sunlight streaming through the window intensified the green depths of her eyes. "You're free to go on as before, if you like."

"That hardly seems fair to Jeff."

"He likes you, and I think a relationship with you would help him as he grows," she said. "But I know you only agreed to be a donor because Lowell pressured you. As far as I'm concerned, you have no obligations."

No obligations. That was what Dirk had always wanted—a life filled with nothing except what he took on voluntarily. He'd realized in retrospect that he hadn't postponed marrying Elena simply because of business opportunities. He hadn't been able to face committing himself permanently to satisfying someone else's needs. The prospect was like being locked inside an airless room, the way he'd felt growing up beneath his father's thumb.

Jeff was different; he hadn't had any say in the arrangements made by grown-ups, and he could hardly be expected to meet his own needs. Besides, being around the boy was more fun than Dirk would have expected.

"I owe him something," he said. "Whether I chose this situation or not, I'm the only father he's got left."

Joni gave him a ghost of a smile. "Herb would enjoy seeing you more often, too. Sure, some kind of holiday schedule would be fine."

"We can work it out over the next few days."

"Great."

They finished their meal with no further discussion. Afterward, Dirk checked the premises again, made sure Joni locked the door behind him, then set off. He had a lot of ground to cover in his investigation and he couldn't afford to delay.

First, however, he paid a visit to Viento del Mar's only car wash. While soapy water cleaned the red paint from his hood, he called one of his assistants in Rome and went over the progress of a new business shipping medicinal herbs from Indonesia to France. He had completed the initial work and turned over day-to-day operations to a manager. Nevertheless, he kept an eye on his projects to make sure everything ran smoothly.

All traces of the paint were gone by the time he tipped the attendant. Whoever had thrown it had either intended more to annoy than to harm or had simply seized whatever paint was at hand. The killer, or someone acting on impulse?

The route to the Peterson estate took Dirk past the Viento del Mar Country Club. From the road, he could see part of the golf course and, behind a stand of trees, the red-tiled roof of the main building.

As a young man, he'd enjoyed having access to a swimming pool, weight room, racquetball courts and other facilities. He'd paid little attention to the gossip, the social climbing or the snobbery.

Now he realized how uncomfortable the setting must have been for Joni, especially after Kim returned from San Francisco. Nevertheless, as Lowell's wife, she might have taken her place if she'd shared the in crowd's values.

But she hadn't. Thank goodness.

He turned from the main road onto winding Pioneer Lane. It snaked through a canyon, working its way upward through heavy brush. A couple of miles along, he angled onto a private driveway. Palm trees lined the route to the one-story Spanish-style mansion. With its courtyard, tile-covered fountain and arched entryway, it reminded him of a Moorish palace.

Behind it lay tennis courts, a five-car garage and a guest cottage used by the three full-time staff members. Since Lowell's death, the main house was unoccupied; Herb had moved out long ago, seeking a more convivial atmosphere in town.

In his will, Lowell had left the house equally to Dirk and Jeff, but neither was ever likely to live there. Dirk hoped he could sell the place to a family that would make good use of it. A family with children...

Unbidden, an image popped into his mind of Jeff sailing a toy boat in the fountain while Joni watched, laughing. How could Lowell have been foolish enough to let them go?

He parked in a shaded turnaround. As he got out, a portly woman in a flowered shirtwaist dress hurried down the front steps. From her stiffly coiffed hair to her polished pumps, there was no mistaking the redoubtable Mrs. Wright.

The housekeeper had nearly reached her station wagon when she became aware of him. She halted abruptly, lost her grip on her purse and snatched it halfway to the ground. "My goodness! You startled me!"

"Sorry." He gave her a friendly grin. "I didn't mean to."

Hired during his mother's final illness when he was twelve, Mrs. Wright had made sure Dirk was ferried to and from school and had a lunch packed each morning. She wasn't the type to get personally involved, and he hadn't wanted her to.

"We're glad to have you back." Composure recovered, she spoke with her customary dignity. "You should tell Cook if you're planning to stay for dinner."

"I'm not moving back," he said. "I need to go through my brother's papers."

"I see." Her expression remained impassive.

"Off to run errands?"

"So to speak." The frown lines deepened in her forehead. "I hope you don't expect me to account for every minute of my day."

Somewhat taken aback by her frostiness, Dirk tried to reassure her. "Considering that you're on the premises almost all the time, certainly not." Mrs. Wright shared the three-bedroom guest house with the groundskeeper and his wife, the cook. "Take as long as you like."

With a nod, she departed. As he let himself into the house, Dirk wondered why Mrs. Wright had become so defensive when he'd only been making conversation. He also wondered why she'd taken a dislike to Joni. Had his sister-in-law's open, frank personality unsettled the housekeeper? Or did Mrs. Wright have something to hide?

He really ought to be careful about becoming paranoid, Dirk chided himself. The housekeeper had always kept her private life to herself.

Even if he hadn't known how much she cared about Lowell, Mrs. Wright was overweight and probably in her sixties. It would take more imagination than he possessed to picture her lurking in the woods at night, let alone overcoming Lowell on Joni's patio.

Dirk paced along a hallway past the oversize, sunken living room. Dark woods and sparse Mediterranean furniture created a cool impression, warmed by colorful throw pillows and wall hangings.

He thought of Joni living here, sharing breakfast with Lowell, bringing home Jeff as a baby. If she'd made any changes to reflect her personality, however, they'd been removed long ago.

Bypassing a large den and another hallway, he

reached the master suite. This had once been his parents' room and then Lowell's, but thanks to the efficient Mrs. Wright, it appeared as impersonal as the public rooms. No hairbrushes bristled on the dressing table. In the entertainment corner, the CDs and laser discs stood neatly in place. Whatever mess the police had made in their search, Mrs. Wright must have cleared it.

Dirk slid open one of the two double closets. Inside, Lowell's clothes hung neatly, the suits and shirts in cleaners' bags, the athletic clothes pressed and placed on hangers. Everything was so tidy, he detected not even a trace of aftershave lotion.

In the second closet, he found two tuxedos in garment bags and rows of expensive leather shoes on racks. Dirk checked for jogging shoes that might have left the tread he'd seen, but there were none.

An office opened off the bedroom. At one time, it had served as his mother's sewing and dressing room, but wood paneling and office furniture had transformed it into a man's hideaway. Inside, Dirk found a desk, a wooden filing cabinet and a leather couch. A top-of-the-line computer and a printer-fax-copier covered the desktop.

Through the blinds, he could see the patch of lawn where his grandfather had long ago erected a swing set and a play fort. They'd been removed during his teen years, but it seemed a shame that Lowell hadn't replaced them for Jeff.

Easing onto the swivel chair, Dirk turned on the computer and searched its memory. Lowell's penchant for organization simplified the job: files from the printing company were grouped in one directory, games in another. The large number of entertainment programs mostly featured a sports theme. Even the preprogrammed

Internet sites turned out to be either business or sports related.

After determining that the files held nothing relevant to his investigation, Dirk switched off the computer and went through the desk. In the top drawer, he noted neatly laid-out pens, pads, a stapler and two pairs of scissors. Below that, he found a few receipts and the latest quarterly reports from mutual funds.

The filing cabinet yielded income-tax forms, financial statements, insurance information and routine correspondence. Nothing useful there, either.

The family's safe had been placed, not very cleverly, behind a painting. After opening it with the combination the family lawyer had given him, Dirk found only a duplicate of Lowell's will alongside a few other legal documents.

With a sense of frustration, he closed it and replaced the painting. What had he hoped to uncover anyway?

Some detail that would help clear Joni, he admitted silently. Or at least something that might sway Mac-Dougall's mind.

But what? If there'd been a bitter dispute of the kind likely to inspire murder, it could hardly have been kept secret in this town. And had Lowell received any threats, he would've turned them over to the police or his lawyer.

The bathroom proved equally sterile; even the cord to the electric shaver was fastidiously coiled. Returning to the bedroom, Dirk sifted through the nightstand but found nothing unusual.

There were some items of jewelry in the top drawer of the dresser, along with neatly folded underwear and T-shirts. The second drawer contained an electric blanket in such pristine condition that it might never have been used. The bottom drawer was empty.

Irrationally, Dirk wished some hint remained of his brother's presence. Whiskers in the sink. A magazine open on the nightstand. Mismatched socks in the drawer.

It was as if Mrs. Wright had removed any sign of Lowell's individuality, he thought with a flash of resentment. The memorial service wasn't even scheduled until Monday afternoon. What was her hurry to tidy up?

But then, he recalled, she'd always dealt with stress by throwing herself into her work. When his mother died, the closet and bathroom had been cleared right after the funeral. He supposed a psychologist might say that such compulsiveness was a way of regaining control when her world went topsy-turvy.

Returning to the top drawer, Dirk examined the jewelry. Those items should go to Jeff, he determined, so he removed a dress watch, a couple of gold tie clasps and a set of silver cuff links. He was about to close the drawer when he decided to feel around the back of it one more time. In a corner, his hand brushed something velvety, and he pulled it out.

It was a small black jeweler's box. Inside, two large diamonds winked from a pair of crescent earrings. A crumpled piece of stiff white paper was wedged to one side. Smoothed out, it proved to be Lowell's business card. A message in his brother's jagged writing said, "Kim. No hard feelings. L."

On the back, in a different hand, was scribbled, "You can't buy me off. You'll pay, but not in money." There was no signature.

So Kim had returned the peace offering with a threat. That was hardly incriminating enough to make her a suspect, though, Dirk reflected as he tucked the velvet box into his pocket. Any woman who'd been dumped might write a note like that.

A glance through the rest of the house uncovered nothing more of interest. His time would be better spent at the printing plant, where round-the-clock shifts worked all weekend. Dirk had a lot of people to interview and documents to examine, especially relating to a publishing venture his brother had planned.

Even if he couldn't learn anything useful about Lowell, he needed to put the place in order. For Jeff's sake. For his son.

BY THE TIME THE OWENSES dropped Jeff at home, Joni had awakened from her nap and started dinner. Dirk wouldn't be eating with them; he'd phoned to say he'd grab a sandwich at the plant.

"What are we having?" Jeff asked as soon as Bobby and his mother drove off. Fred had already left for his regular Saturday-night basketball game. "Oh, good, spaghetti! Mom, you should see our costumes. I mean, they're not done yet, but Mrs. Owens has this pattern…"

He chattered on while Joni stirred the sauce. The pattern did sound perfect, and thanks to Kathryn's skill with a sewing machine, the costumes would probably turn out better than anything they could buy at a store.

Joni did her best to return the Owenses' kindness by writing press releases for Kathryn's garden club and editing the scripts Fred used when calling insurance prospects. Also, last summer, she'd tutored both boys in spelling, a subject given short shrift by their school curriculum.

Still, she would never be able to do as much for the Owenses as they did for her. Whisking Jeff away from the soccer field today, for example. Thanks to them, he hadn't heard Kim's cruel words. *He only married you on the rebound....You cheap, social-climbing little tramp!*

None of it was true. Lowell hadn't married her until two years after Kim took her heart to San Francisco. He'd had plenty of time to recover. As for social climbing, anyone who knew her realized how laughable that accusation was. But a lot of people didn't know her. They made assumptions or they listened to the grapevine.

Dirk's accompanying her to the game might have set their tongues wagging in yet another direction, she supposed. Well, that would pass soon enough when he returned to his work and left Viento del Mar behind.

The prospect of only seeing him once or twice a year left a hollow feeling in her stomach. Or maybe, Joni told herself firmly, she was just hungry.

She set plates of spaghetti and salad on the table. Jeff ran to wash his hands, then scooted his chair close to the table and tucked into the food. Watching him eat, Joni wondered if other people had noted the resemblance to Dirk. She was glad he'd agreed to remain a part of Jeff's life even if it was only for special occasions.

While Jeff cleared the table, she loaded the dishwasher. At his request, she let him mop off the table, although he used so much cleanser that she had to dry it with a towel.

After the nightly ritual of toothbrushing and reading together, she kissed her son good-night and went to watch TV. But she quickly tired of it. Besides, it made her uneasy not to be able to hear any noises from outside.

All day, Joni had avoided thinking about Dirk's discovery of a footprint and a natural blind so close to the house, but in the lengthening silence, she could no longer avoid it. She was still being stalked, probably by the same person who'd murdered Lowell. He might even have been at the soccer game and splashed the paint on Dirk's car, although that act seemed petty compared to murder.

In her anxiety, Joni peeled another strip of polish off a fingernail. She decided to give herself a manicure. Glad to find something to do, she went to the dressing table in the oversize master bathroom and pulled out her manicure set. Soon the piercing scent of acetone filled the air.

Working on something concrete helped focus her thoughts. *Scrub off the polish.* The stalker wasn't some faceless monster. He or she had a name, maybe a job. *Rub hard, all the way to the cuticle.* If she ran through the possibilities systematically, maybe she could figure out who it was. It must either be someone she knew or someone who'd seen her and developed a fixation. A store clerk, a deliveryman, an orderly at the hospital.

She pictured Charlie earlier today, scowling at Dirk. She'd met the coach when soccer practice began in August, not long before the harassment started.

Charlie made a natural suspect. He'd shown an interest in Joni. And he'd been absent today long enough to have splashed paint on Dirk's car. He was also a relative newcomer to town, with no family here.

Yet Joni couldn't help wanting to give him the benefit of the doubt. She knew how it felt to be an outsider and the subject of other people's unwarranted assumptions. Besides, she'd known Charlie such a short time, it was hard to imagine his growing so possessive as to become homicidal.

When she was finished doing her nails, she turned on

the hair dryer, impatient to have them set. A noise from Jeff's room, however, made her switch off the dryer.

The sound came again, a crunch or a scrape. Not from her son's room, but from outside, on the patio.

The stalker.

Anxiety billowed through her. She could barely think.

She should call the police. But...Dirk. Maybe it was Dirk.

He might've come home and decided to walk around the murder scene once more. Contacting the police would not only make Joni look foolish, it might make them less likely to respond in the future.

Taking a deep breath, she moved down the hall. In the utility room, she turned on the outside light and peered through the glass panel. All she could see was a circle of weak illumination.

Then, a twitch of movement—and a gray-striped cat strolled into view. It lowered its head to sniff at something. Curiosity satisfied, it ambled to her rose bed and squatted. Darn that animal! If it wanted to relieve itself, it should use the woods.

Grabbing a broom and a flashlight, Joni hurried out. "Beat it, buster!" For a moment, the cat held its position, regarding her with glowing eyes, then fled.

Joni scanned the yard and called Dirk's name a couple of times before walking to where she could see the driveway, but his car wasn't there. The noise she'd heard must have come from the cat.

About to go inside, she remembered that the animal had been sniffing something, so she trained her flashlight on the patio.

The beam stopped on a dark patch near where she'd fallen Wednesday night. She could have sworn there'd been nothing there earlier today.

Joni edged closer. The patch appeared to be thick, even gooey. Beneath the light, it glistened a dark reddish-brown. Like blood.

It took a moment to register something even more frightening: a swish of leaves from the direction of the blind, then a hard thumping as someone rushed toward her.

A scream welled deep inside, but Joni's throat clamped shut. All that came out was a rasping breath, as if she were strangling.

Chapter Nine

Joni's hands tightened on the broomstick. Fighting tremors of fear, she braced herself with the bristles held straight in front of her.

Into the light eased a slim figure, a woman with straight black hair above an oversize green sweater. "It is me." Celia Lu halted a few feet shy of the broom.

Joni lowered it. "You startled me!" Her breath came shallowly, and her chest constricted. The symptoms of panic refused to abate even though danger no longer threatened.

"Where is your brother-in-law?" her neighbor asked. "Is he not here?"

"He'll be back soon." Feeling suddenly weak, Joni grasped the edge of the glass table. "There's something on the patio. I think it's blood."

Celia produced her own flashlight and inspected the ground. "How disgusting!" She fumbled with something next to the house.

Joni didn't realize what her neighbor was doing until water from a hose swished across the patio. "Wait! Stop!"

The flow halted. "What is wrong? I am cleaning it for you."

"Celia, what if that's human blood? The police might be able to trace the DNA or something."

The older woman stared at her for a moment or two until comprehension dawned. "You think it is killer? I assumed...an animal, perhaps?"

"It might've been left here as a threat," Joni said. "Someone splashed red paint on Dirk's car earlier today."

Celia shuddered. "I am glad I locked my back door. Quickly. We go inside."

It was only when they'd reached the security of the kitchen that Joni began to think clearly again. A stalker might have made that mess, but the cat *had* left dead animals on the patio before. Perhaps this time a large one had managed to drag itself away. She hoped it survived.

"It is good your son sleeps soundly," Celia said. "Or does he stay at a friend's house?"

"He's here." Joni listened but heard no noise from Jeff's room. "That kid could sleep through a nuclear bomb."

"That is healthy, I think."

"Would you like some tea?" Receiving a nod, Joni put the kettle on. While they waited for it to boil, she asked, "Aren't you afraid to go wandering around in the dark, considering what's happened?"

"I forget about danger." Only a fine web of lines near her eyes hinted that Celia must be near fifty. Her habitually unruffled demeanor contributed to the impression of agelessness. "When my husband is not home, I like company. Besides, I hear a rumor that I wished to ask you about. I do not like to rely on—what do you call them? Third parties."

"A rumor?" Joni couldn't imagine where Celia

would pick up gossip about her. But she supposed her neighbor must know other families, some of whom had children at Jeff's school. "What kind of rumor?"

"From the soccer game today." Celia, who as a matter of custom had removed her shoes when she entered the house, perched on one of the kitchen chairs. "That snooty Mrs. DeLong. She was very insulting to you."

"One of your friends overheard?" Joni steeped tea bags in two cups and carried them to the table. "Most people had gone by then."

"My friend—a lady I know from church—caught only a few words. Thank you. Is there any sugar?"

"Of course." Joni provided it, along with a small tin of cookies that she kept for company.

"Delicious," Celia pronounced. "No one likes Mrs. DeLong. She has a very poor character."

Joni wondered to what extent her neighbor had dropped by to seek company and to what extent she was fishing for more gossip to carry back to her friends. It was an uncharitable speculation, she decided, and dismissed it.

Natives of Hong Kong, the Lus had fled before its return to Chinese rule. Mr. Lu held a position with an American bank, so they hadn't suffered economically, but the cultural differences and the isolation must have been stressful.

"If you don't mind my changing the subject," Joni said, "why did you decide to move to Viento del Mar?"

"Perhaps it was foolish. My husband has a long commute. He works in Santa Barbara." After two cookies, the lid was returned to the tin, though not without a certain wistfulness on Celia's part. "He often goes overseas, so he let me pick our home. My cousin lives in town, so I chose here."

Joni hadn't been aware that the Lus had relatives in the area. "I don't think I've met your cousin, have I?"

Celia made a face. "He is a busy man, a dentist. I thought his wife and I would be friends, but she has no time for me. All she wants is for me to baby-sit. I would be glad to do it, but only if we are friends. I am not her free servant!"

Despite the fierce words, Joni could see the sadness in her neighbor's eyes. No wonder the woman sought company; she'd chosen an out-of-the-way place to live in the hopes of being among family, and instead she was often alone.

If Celia hadn't come by Wednesday night, there was no telling how long Joni might have lain dazed in the storm. "Well, her loss is my gain, as we say."

Her neighbor puzzled over the saying for a moment. "I think that is a compliment."

"Definitely."

A smile warmed the usually serious face. "Do not worry. I will watch for this intruder. And if I hear that stuck-up Mrs. DeLong say bad things about you, I will call her many bad names! In Chinese."

Joni laughed. "Thank you."

By the time Dirk came home, the two of them were watching an *I Love Lucy* rerun and laughing out loud. He looked tired but relieved to see her feeling well, and there seemed no point in telling him about the blood, or whatever it had been, until morning.

LYING IN BED ALL NIGHT, knowing Joni was only a few dozen feet away, set Dirk's body throbbing.

He'd been struck by her natural sensuality last night when she came to the door with her face aglow from watching a comedy. Warm light seemed to shine from within, and he'd become intensely aware of the softness of her skin and the slimness of her body in the clinging jeans and T-shirt.

Exhaustion from a long evening of evaluating the printing company's financial status had made it easy to fall asleep. The problem came when Dirk awoke about two in the morning and, en route to the bathroom, heard her easy breathing.

The house radiated Joni's essence. It brought out, almost painfully, the demands of his own masculinity. He nearly walked down the hall and opened her door to watch her as she slept. Only the knowledge that it would be an invasion of privacy held him back.

Dirk wasn't sure what he wanted or expected from this woman. To go to bed with Joni and then leave would hurt her. And, possibly, him, as well.

He knew what he was: a modern-day adventurer. The prospect of a home and family tantalized him, but the wildness of his own nature would never allow him to stay in one place for long.

Why was he suddenly yearning for something he couldn't have? Perhaps, he decided as he tossed sleeplessly, it was a reaction to Lowell's death. A sense of the past slipping away, of human connections vanishing.

Yet he'd just discovered the greatest human connection of all. He had a child.

The worst thing he could do, Dirk reflected, would be to dally with the boy's mother. Their son needed them both.

He finally dozed, only to be yanked from unconsciousness as Jeff bounced into the den. Prying one eye open, Dirk groped for his watch, then sat up sharply. "Eight o'clock? We'll be late for church."

The Petersons traditionally attended Viento del Mar

Highlands Church. The service had started at nine o'clock ever since he could remember. Although Dirk wasn't religious, the church was as much a social as a spiritual center for the town's movers and shakers. Furthermore, he knew Herb expected them to attend.

"It's seven." Jeff clicked on his video-game system.

"Eight," Dirk grumbled.

The boy pointed to the digital display on the VCR. It read 7:02.

"It's wrong," Dirk said. "This watch keeps time in every zone around the globe. It doesn't vary by more than one minute per year, and it beeps if the battery runs low."

"Does it also beep when we go off daylight savings time?" Joni asked from the doorway.

The last Sunday in October. He groaned. "I forgot."

"I nearly did, too," she admitted. "I woke up last night and adjusted the time in my room and Jeff's. The VCR resets itself."

"We're not late for church after all," Jeff said. "Aren't you glad?"

Dirk supposed he was.

They ate waffles from the freezer served with plenty of syrup. "Sometimes I make pancakes from scratch," Joni said apologetically as Dirk helped Jeff cut his food. "I'm just not up to it yet."

"Still hurting?" Dirk regarded her with concern. "Maybe you should stay home for a few more days."

"I'd rather not, but I do tire easily." She finished a bite of breakfast. "Lowell's memorial service is at four o'clock tomorrow, isn't it? Maybe Jeff and I should both stay home."

To Dirk's surprise, the boy shook his head vigorously. "Can't you pick me up after school?"

"You're ready to go back?" he asked.

The boy gave him a puzzled frown. "Yeah, sure. They're having pizza for lunch. Besides, Bobby and I always play handball at recess."

The boy's reaction seemed odd, but perhaps he lacked the perspective to realize how permanent death was. At age eight, Dirk supposed he'd have been worried about missing pizza and handball, too.

He glanced at Joni for her reaction. "Do you think it's wise?"

She regarded her son thoughtfully. "If he stays around here, he'll only mope. It's best for him to stick with his routine."

Dirk supposed she was right. He found it easier to deal with his grief by taking action, and Jeff, too, might feel better if he kept busy. "Does he ride the bus?"

"Usually I drop him off on my way to the hospital," Joni said. "The day-care center picks him up afterward, and I collect him there when I finish work."

"I'll drive him in the morning," Dirk said. "You stay home."

To his relief, she agreed. Although only a fading purple bruise remained visible along her temple, Joni's fragile air brought home the fact that she'd been seriously hurt. By the time she applied makeup and dressed for church, however, she gave no sign of being ill. In fact, Dirk thought as he helped her into his car, his sister-in-law was likely to turn heads.

She'd chosen a smoke-gray suit with a dark green blouse that made her eyes glint like emeralds. Freshly washed and fragrant, her blond hair had been twisted into a knot, leaving a fringe around her face.

Jeff wore a navy blazer, a white button-down shirt and

tan pants. He looked, Dirk realized with a start, like a miniature version of himself.

When they reached the church, they found quite a few cars already there. Another family entered the large, hushed foyer just as they did. Sideways glances and a deliberate turning away made it clear that they were snubbing Joni. Anger simmered inside Dirk. If he and Herb were willing to give her the benefit of the doubt, who were these people to pass judgment?

As the newcomers disappeared into the sanctuary, a door opened from the adjacent multipurpose room. Out came Mrs. Wright, who started when she caught sight of the new arrivals.

"Mr. Peterson!" The housekeeper, who had joined the church years ago after attending with the family, regarded him anxiously. "Have you seen Mrs. DeLong?"

"Kim?" He hadn't realized the two were even acquainted. "No, why?"

"She's chairman of the hospitality committee." Mrs. Wright gave Jeff a brief smile before continuing. "She was supposed to bring doughnuts for the reception after the service, but she's not here."

The hospitality committee was the domain of the town's social set, with an occasional addition like Mrs. Wright to handle any work the others found tedious. "Anyone can have a flat tire," Dirk pointed out.

"Yes, but she *does* have a car phone." The woman shrugged. "Well, there's nothing I can do about it now." She marched off, still without a word to Joni.

"Boy, that's awful," Jeff said.

If the housekeeper's attitude was affecting his son, Dirk would have to speak to the woman about it. "What is?" he asked cautiously.

"They don't have any doughnuts. I like the jelly ones best. What about you?"

"Chocolate," Dirk said. "Joni?"

"Lemon filled." She chuckled. "For once, I hope Kim shows up."

Inside, Herb had saved seats near the front. When Jeff ran to his great-grandfather and hugged him, Dirk could see tears glistening in the old man's eyes.

Throughout the service, the room seemed to bristle with undercurrents. Even the minister, a young man who'd been hired after Dirk moved away, made a reference to their shared grief at the loss of a valued friend.

The reception afterward proved short, due to the absence of refreshments. Kim DeLong had not arrived.

"It isn't like her," Mrs. Wright clucked as she poured punch into paper cups.

Kim's friend from the soccer game fussed over a centerpiece of dried flowers. "She did say she hadn't found a costume yet for the Frightful Nightful." That was the country club's annual Halloween party. "Maybe she decided to make a shopping trip to L.A."

"And forgot about the doughnuts?" the housekeeper sniffed. "She should have called someone."

Jeff kept darting to the hallway in hopes of witnessing the arrival of the pastries. At his insistence, Joni went with him to peer out the front door.

Herb steered Dirk into a corner. "What have you found?" he asked without preamble.

"I don't think Joni killed Lowell, and I don't believe he was stalking her. But I haven't got a clue who is."

"Is? Present tense?" His grandfather's brows knitted in alarm.

"Very present tense." Dirk described the duplicate

knife, the footprint in the yard and the red paint on his car.

"What do the police think?"

"I've persuaded them to hold off filing charges for the time being," Dirk said. "But I don't think they're eager to complicate their case."

"If their evidence isn't airtight, the lawyer I'm going to hire will mop up the courtroom with them," Herb growled.

Dirk chuckled at his grandfather's ferocity. Despite his heart condition, the man would go to any lengths to defend his family.

When Joni and Jeff returned, they invited Herb to picnic with them at Del Mar Park, but he declined. "Just be careful," he said in parting.

An hour later, Dirk and Joni had changed into casual clothes and were finishing their take-out fried chicken at a picnic table while Jeff scampered off to play. He didn't know the other two children at the playground, but soon they were all running and whooping together.

"He makes friends easily," Dirk observed. "He's more like Lowell than me in that respect."

"Or me, either. I think he takes after Herb," Joni said. "Listen, I need to tell you something."

He listened to her description of the blood, or whatever it had been, on the patio. "Did you look out there this morning?"

"There was a trace of brown along the edge of the patio, but it might have been left from Wednesday," she said.

"It didn't appear to be red paint?"

"Too brown and too thick."

"Since we're playing show-and-tell, I'd like you to see this." From his pocket, Dirk pulled out the black velvet jeweler's box. He'd been carrying it with him, uneasy at leaving it anywhere else. "Lowell's kiss-off gift to Kim."

Joni read the note. "Everybody knew she was furious. It's the kind of threat people make all the time."

"But usually not to people who get killed," he pointed out.

Sunlight played across her face as she rested her chin on one palm. In contrast to earlier this morning, a healthy pink flushed her cheeks, and threads of reddish-gold glinted in the hair that had pulled loose from its knot. "Kim would certainly have a motive to harass me. But I can't see her overpowering Lowell."

"Not to mention that the shoe print I saw in the blind was man-size," Dirk noted. As the events at church this morning ran through his mind, he added, "By the way, was Mrs. Wright always this chilly toward you?"

"She used to acknowledge me, but not by much," she said.

"Any idea why you two didn't get along?"

"It wasn't so bad right after we were married. Then a couple of years before the divorce, I stepped on her toes, I guess." Joni pursed her lips at the memory. "I asked her where she went in the middle of the day. She would leave for several hours, two or three times a week."

"Did she tell you?"

"No, she blew up. She said no one had ever questioned her integrity before," Joni said. "I didn't mean to criticize. It just struck me as odd."

He recalled how the housekeeper had bristled yesterday when he asked if she was running errands. "What did Lowell say?"

"He told me Mrs. Wright was like a member of the

family and she could come and go as she pleased.'' Joni's voice tightened as she recounted the rebuke. ''Do you think I was out of line?''

''Considering you were her employer, I wouldn't say so. If she'd made special arrangements with Lowell, he should've advised you.'' Why *had* the woman been so touchy anyway? And where did she go?

Jeff and the other children jumped onto the swings and launched themselves into the air, whooping with glee. Eight years old. Dirk couldn't even remember how it had felt to be that age. He wondered what his son had been like as an infant or a toddler. When he took his first step. On his first day at school.

''I've missed so much,'' he said.

''You found more than the police did.'' Joni reached across the table to pick a leaf off his hair.

The touch of her fingers heated his scalp. ''I meant about Jeff, not the investigation. Like his birth. And birthdays. All the special times I wasn't there.''

''If you'd known he was your son, would it have made any difference?'' she asked.

Dirk had to admit the truth. ''I suppose not. I did what my brother asked, then put it out of my mind. Maybe that was noble or maybe it was selfish. Nothing I can do about it now.''

''June seventeenth,'' she said.

''What's that?''

''His birthday.'' She smiled. ''We'll be expecting you next year.''

''I wouldn't miss it.'' At the far edge of the playground, a shadow moved in a thicket of tall bushes. Under the circumstances, Dirk was on permanent alert. ''Any idea who that might be?''

Joni followed his gaze. ''I can't tell.''

"What's on the far side of those bushes?"

"A soccer field. We practice there on Wednesday afternoons, in fact."

If any teams were using the field now, they'd be making plenty of noise, Dirk thought. He heard nothing beyond the three children on the playground.

"I'll go check it out." Forcing himself to pretend disinterest, he strolled toward the field.

The shadow shifted as he approached, then vanished. Quickening his pace, Dirk loped into the thicket. A branch snagged his sweater, and by the time he tore free, he could see a man's figure vanishing across the small slope that separated the low-lying park from the street beyond.

Dirk broke into a run. He had no reason to connect this onlooker to Lowell's murder, but he'd feel better if he knew who the guy was. By the time Dirk topped the rise, he saw nothing but an empty sidewalk, a residential neighborhood and a scattering of parked cars.

He had left Joni alone at the picnic table. Suppose the intruder doubled back? Unwilling to risk searching for the man, Dirk returned to the playground.

"No luck," he said.

Shivering, Joni wrapped her arms around herself. She'd worn a lavender sweater, not heavy enough for the cool October breeze.

"We could go home," Dirk suggested.

"No. Jeff's enjoying himself. He needs to release some of his grief and tension."

He wasn't going to let her catch cold no matter how cautious he intended to be, so Dirk sat beside Joni and drew her against his chest. Her trembling eased, even as fire ignited inside his own body. "Better?" he asked gruffly.

"Much better," she whispered.

They nestled together, watching Jeff and his new friends play pirates on a jungle gym. As heat flowed between them, the floral scent of her shampoo proved a heady perfume.

Just sitting there, his arms wrapped around her, was an intensely sensual experience. It was a rare beautiful moment as they silently watched their son play.

An hour later, Jeff's friends scampered off to join their parents. Reluctantly, Dirk conceded it was time to go.

"Maybe we can see them again sometime," Jeff said. "Andy and Maggy come here almost every Sunday. Could we come back next week, Mom?"

"We can try," Joni said.

"Uncle Dirk?"

"If I'm still—yes, sure." He wouldn't be gone that soon, would he? Dirk tried not to think about all the Sundays after that. The other afternoons that would pass as Jeff grew, the thousands of moments he wouldn't share.

At home, to spare the front carpet from Jeff's sandy shoes, they went to the back door. Dirk, watching for any sign of the stalker, noticed a brick askew in a built-in planter alongside the house.

"Did you do that?" he asked, pointing.

Joni stopped. "Oh, my goodness. That's where I hide the spare key!"

"Jeff? Did you move that this morning?"

The boy shook his head.

Joni bent to examine the brick. "Don't touch it!" Dirk said. "There might be fingerprints."

"I want to know if the key's here!" Dropping to her knees, she pulled the brick out and scooped up a small object. "Thank goodness!"

Could there be some innocent explanation for the loose brick? "When's the last time you took it out?"

"I can't remember," Joni said.

"Thursday." They turned toward Jeff. "Mrs. Owens took it out," he explained. "Remember, I had to get some stuff to sleep over at Grampa's house."

"That's right. She brought me clean clothes, too." Joni's voice quavered as she added, "But the brick wasn't like this yesterday or I'd have noticed."

"Who else knows about the key?" Dirk asked.

"Just Herb."

And anyone who's been watching the house from the blind, he thought grimly. "I'll get someone at the printshop to come out and change the locks. For the time being, please stop hiding a key."

"Don't worry," she said fervently.

He insisted on going inside first, listening, watching, feeling for changes in air pressure. The only thing he noticed was a slow, creeping sensation on his skin. Dirk had learned to trust his gut feelings, and they were shouting, *Intruder!*

"If it's the stalker, I'm sure he's left some indication he was here," he said. "He'd want to flaunt himself."

Joni turned to Jeff. "You stay right here in the hall while we look."

"Not by myself!" he protested.

"Both of you go into the kitchen and wait by the phone," Dirk said. "Be ready to call 911."

He poked through the house, every sense on edge. Even ordinary noises seemed sharper and the smells harsher than usual. However, no drawers had been ripped open and nothing appeared damaged. But there was a final test.

Thanks to his years in security work, Dirk always

made small folds in the edges of his clothing that would fall open if they were disturbed. He opened the end table in the den and examined his clothing without moving it. The folds were gone.

Someone had poked through his things. At the discovery, the hairs bristled on the back of his neck.

As Dirk straightened, he noticed a hint of orange beneath the table. On closer inspection, it revealed itself to be a small ruffled ball of orange and purple. Squatting, he plucked it from the carpet. It was instantly recognizable as a fringed pom-pom pin, the kind Kim DeLong had been wearing the last time Dirk saw her.

Chapter Ten

Detective MacDougall brought a crime-scene crew to the house. Joni wasn't thrilled about the mess they made, but she was glad that at least he was taking the break-in seriously.

Or so she hoped until he reported that the investigators had found nothing aside from the pom-pom pin. They could only assume that the intruder must have worn gloves and put plastic bags over his shoes.

She could read the unspoken tag line in his eyes. *If there really was an intruder.*

"I'm afraid we don't have a lot to go on," the detective growled as the team finished its work.

"What did you learn about the red paint?" Dirk asked.

"It's a brand the hardware store sells, although they don't remember anyone buying that shade recently," MacDougall said. "Too bad your neighbor hosed down the brown stuff on the patio. We couldn't find anything to test."

They stood on the front porch, watching for a machinist who worked the weekend shift at Peterson Printing. Dirk had arranged for him to rekey all the locks as soon as the police finished.

"What about the pin?" she asked. "And the threatening note Kim DeLong wrote to Lowell?"

MacDougall's face had a pouchy look, possibly from being called out three times on a weekend, or maybe from frustration. "The booster club sells those pins at games. As for the note, it doesn't prove anything."

She hated to admit it, but he was right. Their evidence didn't add up to much.

"I have one more question for you," MacDougall went on. "I didn't realize yesterday, Mr. Peterson, that you were staying on the premises. Don't you think that raises certain questions about your objectivity, if nothing else?"

She saw a muscle jump in Dirk's jaw. The detective's implication was unfair, and yet...

Since Dirk moved into the house, she'd been subliminally aware of him even when they were apart. The low timbre of his voice echoed in her bones; she awoke with vague memories of dreams filled with caresses and whispers. In the shower, when she passed the creamy soap across her skin, she could almost feel his presence, watching, touching, helping.

Could she be objective? Could he?

"My nephew and his mother are being stalked on the same property where my brother was murdered," Dirk retorted. "Until we can get a security system installed, I'm staying. Unless you're offering to post a round-the-clock guard?"

"We're a small department. We don't have that kind of manpower."

"Or I could move them both to the Peterson estate," he said. "Joni?"

Until these latest developments, the desire not to uproot Jeff had tipped the balance in favor of staying here.

Now that someone had invaded the house, she wasn't sure.

Joni pictured the meandering mansion in its isolated setting. There would be plenty of room for them, but they'd have to contend with a hostile housekeeper, keys floating around in the hands of servants and no neighbors close enough to hear a scream.

She supposed she could move to a motel, but that idea didn't appeal to her, either. Flimsy doors, people coming and going outside and nowhere for her son to play.

"I'm staying put," she said. "This stalker will find me no matter where I go."

Dirk accepted her decision as if he'd expected it. To the detective, he said, "Will you talk to Mrs. DeLong about her pin?"

MacDougall stiffened. "I'm sure that will be part of the investigation."

He wasn't going to dig very hard, and Joni knew why. The detective didn't believe there was a stalker. In his mind, she had killed Lowell, and now she or Dirk, or both, were trying to plant doubt about her guilt.

Dirk must have been thinking along the same lines because after the police left and Jeff went to his room, he said, "I'm afraid that once MacDougall talks to Kim and she denies everything, he's going to turn his evidence over to the D.A."

"You think they'll charge me?" she asked numbly. "Why?"

"Because people don't like to repeat their mistakes," he said.

"What do you mean?"

"I've been doing some research on the Internet." Dirk led the way into the living room, where he stood at the window watching the driveway below. "Trying to get background on everyone who's relevant to this case. That includes the D.A."

From his tone, she suspected she wouldn't like what he'd found. "What did you learn?"

"A few years ago, he declined to file charges in a self-defense case," he said. "The suspect was a former boxer. He said his wife came at him with a knife and he punched her too hard.

"A few months later, they found out he'd previously killed a girlfriend under identical circumstances in another state and gotten off with the same excuse. By that time, he'd disappeared. There was a big stink about letting a murderer get away with it."

"So the D.A. won't back off unless I have ironclad proof I didn't do it." Joni's spirits sank. She didn't even feel strong enough to go back to work yet; how was she going to face a jury?

"Herb's got a top-ranking lawyer in mind," Dirk said. "If you like, I'll engage him right away so he can put his investigative team to work."

"I can't deal with any more people right now." Joni wrapped her arms around herself protectively. "You're the only help I want."

He rubbed his hands lightly along her shoulders. The friction lit a flame deep within her. "I may be doing you more harm than good. Now that he knows I'm staying here, MacDougall's going to discount anything I come across."

"I don't care. I'm glad you're with me." Tears threatened to shatter her composure, but she forced them back. "Dirk, I'm barely holding myself together. I don't know what's wrong. I'm not usually a wimp."

"You've been operating on automatic since Wednesday night.'' His fingers feathered along her neck beneath her loosened hair. ''The trauma is catching up to you.''

''Just don't leave. I don't care what MacDougall thinks.''

''I'm not going anywhere.'' He moved closer, curving around her, lowering his face to hers. In another heartbeat, their lips would meet.

Outside, a vehicle downshifted as it ascended the driveway. A Peterson Printing van, she saw from the corner of her eye.

Unwillingly, Dirk released her. ''We seem to have the world's worst timing. Tell you what. Tonight, I'm building a fire in the fireplace. Got any hot dogs?''

She smiled. ''There's a package in the fridge.''

''Any long skewers?''

''Not only that,'' she said, ''I've got marshmallows.''

''A woman after my own heart.'' The words lingered in the air as he went to meet the machinist.

THERE WERE MORE LOCKS than Dirk had realized—front door, back door, the door between the house and the garage, plus a side door from the garage to the yard.

The workman adjusted them all and handed him a set of keys. ''I hope that takes care of the problem, Mr. Peterson.''

''I'll see that you're paid extra for your time,'' Dirk said.

The man, a grizzled fellow who appeared to spend most of his spare time outdoors, shook his head. ''I don't need no extra pay,'' he said. ''What I want, like most of the guys, is for you to keep the company in the family.''

''We haven't made a decision about that.'' Dirk wasn't surprised to learn that the staff had been speculating about the future. Their jobs might be at stake after all. "Unfortunately, there won't be anyone in the family who could run the place until Jeff grows up."

"Unless, well, unless you was to stay on." The man braced himself against his van. "I don't guess it's as excitin' as what you regularly do. But your brother was talkin' about startin' up his own publishing imprint. We was lookin' forward to seein' what he'd do."

"He mentioned it to me on the phone recently, as a matter of fact." Lowell, his voice brimming with enthusiasm, had suggested they work together on lining up big-name experts to write high-tech and business-oriented books, then market the imprint internationally. It sounded feasible, but Dirk assumed the publishing project had died with Lowell.

His own specialty was establishing new projects in developing nations, not running them day to day. He only stuck around until a company got off the ground.

He knew better, however, than to cut off his options. "It's still up in the air," he said. "Thanks for your input."

"Any time, Mr. Peterson." After a firm handshake, the man climbed into his van.

As he drove away, Jeff came out of the house dribbling a ball. "Hey, Uncle Dirk, want to play handball?"

Dirk felt he could use a workout, and it was a good chance to spend time with his son. "Sure."

Whacking the ball against the garage door and chasing it soon had him breathing hard. A lot harder than Jeff. Considering that the kid had run all over the playground earlier that afternoon, his stamina was impressive.

"You're quite an athlete," Dirk observed as Jeff returned a difficult serve.

"Dad says I take after him."

The ball flew into some bushes. Dirk loped over and collected it. "Lowell was a good sportsman."

"Yeah." The little boy drooped, and Dirk realized his use of the past tense had been a reminder of Lowell's death. "I'll never be as good as him, though."

Dirk put an arm around his son's shoulders. "I don't see why not. Being an athlete runs in the family. Did you know my father was the star of the high school basketball team?"

"No," the boy said, "I didn't."

Donald had died in his mid-fifties, before his only grandson was conceived. Unlike Herb, he'd refused to obey the doctor's orders to diet, exercise and quit smoking.

"Your great-grandfather was a ballplayer, too," Dirk said. "Herb led his team to two basketball trophies. I bet you could, too, if you wanted to."

The child's face brightened. Such keen blue eyes and such an open, joyful expression. Joni had done a wonderful job of raising him.

With a pang, Dirk wondered whether Herb's proximity and his own occasional visits would be enough masculine support to guide the boy into manhood. Even if they were enough for Jeff, did he himself really want to miss these years with the only son he might ever have?

He refused to yield to impulse. The worst thing he could do was to promise more than he could deliver.

"Want to play some more?" Jeff asked.

Dirk gestured toward a pile of logs. "How about helping me build a fire instead?"

"Could we really?"

"I promised your mom we'd have a wienie roast for

dinner," he said. "We'll have to be careful not to set the house ablaze, though."

"We can roast hot dogs in the fireplace?" The boy whooped. "Dad would never have gone for something like that!"

"Your dad probably had more sense than I do," Dirk muttered, but he was human enough to enjoy the compliment.

INSIDE THE GRATE, sparks snapped and leaped from a log. On the brick hearth lay blackened skewers, testament to a merry meal of hot dogs and marshmallows.

Joni lay back among the cushions she'd pulled from the couch. Jeff had gone to bed half an hour ago while, nearby, Dirk watched the fire through half-closed eyes. Her sense of contentment wouldn't last, she knew. That made her treasure it all the more.

"A penny for your thoughts." Lying on the carpet, she could feel Dirk's baritone voice ripple through the underlying boards.

Half-formed ideas sprang out before she even knew what she intended to say. "I have the oddest feeling that everything will come to a head by Thursday."

"Thursday?" he echoed. "Halloween?"

"Also my birthday," she admitted. "The big three-oh."

"Ah." Dirk stretched lazily along his cushions. "I remember my thirtieth birthday. Some friends took me to dinner in Rome."

"That sounds glamorous."

"Rome is more friendly than glamorous," he said. "We had a traveling party, from the restaurant to a nightclub, picking up more people at every stage. People we knew, or thought we knew, or who said witty things in passing, or who laughed at our jokes. I felt like a college student again.''

Through the fire tangoed filaments of red and yellow, blue and black. ''I never had that kind of carefree experience,'' Joni admitted. ''I wish I had.''

''I needed it.'' Dirk knit his hands behind his head. ''I had to get away from here.''

''Why?'' she asked. ''I know you and Lowell didn't get along, but he would never say why.''

''Dad pitted us against each other,'' he said. ''I guess it was his way of trying to spur me to be the kind of kid he wanted me to be, and I was too stubborn to yield. Lowell sure enjoyed needling me.''

''He could be very cruel.'' She'd learned that all too well from her own experience.

''When we were little, I adored him.'' A touch of bitterness laced his words. ''So when we were teenagers and he began taunting me, I supposed he must be right, that I really was inferior. It hurt so much that I couldn't deal with it, so I hid my feelings. I didn't even fight back.''

''Not ever?'' she probed.

''Not until my senior year in high school,'' he said. ''Lowell came home from college and found out I'd taken up boxing. I was doing well at it, too, which galled him.''

''Did he box?'' Joni recalled a scar alongside her ex-husband's eye; she'd asked about it, but he'd brushed the question aside.

''No, but he didn't like seeing me succeed at sports. I guess it threatened his position as the brother who was better at everything,'' Dirk said.

She waited, hoping that he'd go on. After a moment's reflection, he did.

"One afternoon at the club, he and some of his friends started giving me a hard time," Dirk said. "Mostly it was Lowell. Calling me names, shoving me. He challenged me to a boxing match. I knew my coach wouldn't approve, but I'd had enough."

"You two fought?" she asked. "Where?"

"We found an exercise room that wasn't being used," he said. "Put on the gloves and went at each other. Lowell lacked experience, but he was bigger than me."

"He won?" Joni hugged her knees. She could almost see the two brothers squaring off; hear the catcalls of Lowell's friends; smell the fighters' sweat.

"He landed more blows than I did although they didn't do much damage," Dirk said. "He told me I was a loser and I'd always be a loser. I told him to quit acting like a jerk and that I'd had enough. When I started to leave, he suddenly swung around and socked me in the gut. I wasn't expecting it."

Joni flinched. "He cheated?"

"He wanted total and absolute victory, and I wouldn't give it to him, so he took it any way he could." Dirk grimaced.

"Were you badly hurt?"

"I could hardly breathe. Then I got mad," he said. "I've heard of people seeing red, but I never knew it could be literally true. Well, it is. I felt this rage, years and years of it that had been bottled up. I don't remember what happened, except that I attacked him with everything I was worth."

"So that's how he got the scar," she guessed. "Next to his eye."

Dirk nodded. "I might've hurt him even worse if his friends hadn't pulled me off. I got loose and went at him again until Lowell had to turn tail and flee. He hated me for humiliating him, and I figured he owed me an apology. That was fifteen years ago.''

''I'm sorry you never had a chance to reconcile,'' Joni said. ''Lowell must've realized that was the biggest mistake he ever made.''

''No, it wasn't.'' Dirk's blue gaze burrowed into her. ''His biggest mistake was falling in love and then being too stupid to hold on to the most precious thing in his life.''

The intensity of his stare held her motionless. It flooded her with a delicious sense of her own femininity, a sensation Lowell had all but destroyed when he rejected her to have an affair.

She could scarcely breathe, and she didn't know why until she realized that she wanted desperately for Dirk to hold her. A voice inside warned that she shouldn't yield to this weakness. She didn't care. Wasn't it worth the risk to have something precious even if she couldn't keep it?

Whatever lay ahead, Joni couldn't think about it now. The only reality was the sheen of firelight on Dirk's bronzed skin and the inviting warmth of his smile. Without conscious intent, she shifted toward him.

He met her halfway, one hand catching her waist, the other cupping her cheek. Their mouths came together, tongue to tongue. They sank onto the pillows, their legs entwined. After holding back for so long, she arched wildly against him. Wherever they touched, pleasure sprang up, so powerful it ached.

His shoulders rippled beneath her hands. His mouth caught hers again, ravaging and teasing. Her breasts yielded beneath the hard pressure of his chest, and her nipples sprang erect, daring him to take more.

She'd always felt her rangy, boyish body was awkward. But not with Dirk. Angles melted and what had been stiff became molten; she dissolved into him.

His breathing roughened as his hands slipped beneath her sweater. He pulled it up, and fire licked across her breasts as he tasted them. Desire took tangible shape, the shape of flames. Hungrily, Joni loosened Dirk's belt, wanting all of him.

His movements stopped. She felt his head brush her chest, the hair tickling her sensitized nipples. When he pulled away, a chill rushed to take his place. In the flickering light, Dirk sat up. His face was flushed, and he was breathing rapidly.

Joni knew the moment had passed. There would be no more lovemaking, and yet her body defied her with its need. How could she gather her scattered, overheated molecules back into their ordinary shape?

"I can't begin to tell you how difficult this is." Raw emotion layered his voice. "Joni, don't ever think I don't want you. But I would only hurt you."

"How can you be so sure?" she asked.

"I loved a woman once." His voice sounded far away. "I wasn't there when she needed me. She was a bodyguard, like me, and she got killed."

No wonder he gave the impression of nursing a darkness inside. "It couldn't have been your fault."

"If I'd been the right kind of man, she wouldn't have gone on that assignment," he said. "And I'm still the same man I was then, Joni. I have the same needs, and they'll take me away from here."

She wanted to argue that she didn't care, yet she knew it wasn't true. Maybe in time he would change, but she wasn't foolish enough to count on that. She had a child to take care of, and a community to face that already thought the worst of her. The last thing she needed was a dead-end love affair.

He reached for her hand. "It's time we went to bed."

"I wish that were an invitation," she couldn't help saying.

"So do I."

Her body hummed defiantly as he helped her to her feet and put the cushions away. Joni collected the skewers and took them into the kitchen.

They'd gone to the edge tonight, she thought. She couldn't help wondering what lay beyond it.

It was hard to accept that she might never find out.

ON THE AFTERNOON of Lowell's burial, clouds glowered over the Viento del Mar Memorial Park, which was located on the far side of downtown, west of Canyon Vista Road. The planned memorial service had been changed to a funeral at the last minute when the coroner released his body.

Joni wasn't sure whether, as Lowell's ex-wife and suspected killer, she ought to attend. Jeff needed to be there, however, and she wouldn't let him go without her. To wear black seemed presumptuous, so she chose a navy outfit. She and Dirk collected Jeff at school and met Herb at the memorial park.

People filled the chapel and spilled out the rear and side doors. The size of the crowd surprised her until Dirk explained that he'd given the printing staff time off to attend, and Herb added that he'd notified the local radio station.

Inside, flowers covered the dais and the gleaming closed casket. As she walked along the aisle, Joni saw heads turn and heard whispering. The Peterson Printing employees were keeping their expressions neutral. But the country-club set was a different story: tight mouths, narrow eyes and loud voices.

"How dare she come!"

"What a lot of nerve!"

"I'm surprised they haven't locked her up yet!"

Dirk tucked Joni's hand into the crook of his elbow. She guessed from his angry expression that he was weighing the effect of these remarks not only on her, but also on Jeff.

Fortunately, Herb was filling the boy's ears with a running commentary on the types of flowers. Joni doubted her son even heard the rude remarks.

It surprised her not to see Kim DeLong among the mourners. It wasn't like the woman to miss a chance to make her presence felt. A few hospital workers had come, including Basil. Even Detective MacDougall had arrived, lingering near the side door where he could survey the assembly. She wondered whom or what he expected to find.

Dirk escorted her to the front row, which was reserved for family. Already seated there, in a black dress and black hat, Mrs. Wright stiffened when she caught sight of the newcomers. The housekeeper nodded to Herb and Dirk, then resumed facing straight ahead.

Ten minutes later, the service began. Joni registered vaguely that the minister talked about Lowell's dedication to the community and his love for his son.

Jeff squirmed, trying to see the other mourners. At eight years old, he couldn't be expected to grasp the implications of a funeral.

Dirk stood up to say a few words about his thorny relationship with his brother and how they'd hoped to reconcile. Herb spoke about how Lowell had been changing and reassessing his values. No one mentioned the circumstances of his death.

Joni knew that Dirk had contemplated speaking out on her behalf, but she'd urged him not to. This was a time for people who had known Lowell all his life to come together in celebrating and mourning him. It was not a court of law in which to present her defense.

The burial was to be private, and after the service, only she, Herb, Dirk, the pastor and Jeff went to the grave site. Joni was grateful to be away from the disapproving gazes of so many people.

The newer section of the cemetery had the peaceful air of a country garden, with low trees scattered over its rolling lawns. Memorial plaques lay flat on the ground, in contrast to an older section, where headstones towered.

Lowell's marker wasn't ready yet; there was only the hole for the casket. With so little time to make arrangements, they hadn't lined up any pallbearers, so a couple of cemetery workers transported the casket from the chapel and lowered it into the ground.

"Is Daddy really in there?" Jeff asked.

"Just his body," Herb said. "His spirit is free."

"Is he here?" The boy gazed around hopefully.

Joni exchanged troubled glances with Dirk. She wanted Jeff to feel that his father was close by but not to have unrealistic expectations.

"His love is here," Dirk said after a moment. "For you." He ruffled Jeff's hair.

With the casket in place, Dirk tossed down the customary handful of earth. The pastor read a passage from the Bible, and then it was over.

Joni felt grateful for the leaden sky as they walked back to the car. A sunny day wouldn't have felt right.

In the parking lot, one figure stood waiting for them—
the detective. From the set of his jaw, he didn't have
good news. Joni wondered if he were going to arrest her.
Couldn't he at least wait until they left the cemetery?

When they came closer, MacDougall said, "I don't
suppose any of you have heard from Kim DeLong?"

Heads shook. "I didn't see her at the service," Joni
said. "I wondered where she was."

"No one's seen her since Saturday afternoon," the
detective said. "She disappeared right after she talked
to the two of you."

Chapter Eleven

"Are you implying a connection, Detective?" Dirk demanded.

MacDougall's pouchy eyes barely blinked. "Not necessarily. One of her friends saw her get into her car and drive off. We assume she arrived at home since her car is there. But she isn't."

Joni remembered a comment at church. "Could she have gone out of town?"

"Possible but unlikely." The man studied each of their faces in turn. "Unless someone gave her a ride." The nearest public airport was more than twenty miles away in Santa Barbara.

"We hope Mrs. DeLong turns up safe," Herb said dryly, "but right now, we've just buried my grandson. If you have nothing further to add, Officer, we'd like to leave."

"Sorry about the timing." But MacDougall didn't look sorry.

Dirk glared at the man's back as he departed. "I wonder how hard he's tried to find Kim. The police around here aren't terribly thorough."

He exchanged glances with his grandfather. "Well?" Herb prompted.

"I guess I'd better put in some calls to people who might've seen her," Dirk said. "I ought to be able to track down some of her friends from San Francisco. Also find out whether she's used a credit card the past couple of days, although I'm sure the police have already done that."

"I wouldn't put it past the woman to hide out just to get attention," his grandfather muttered.

Joni thought about the pom-pom pin Dirk had found in her house. Was it possible Kim had gone off the deep end and was lying in wait?

It would almost be a relief to be able to give the stalker a name and a face. Yet she had a hard time seeing Kim DeLong in that role. Kim might be vicious, but she was no monster.

"I need to use the computer at the office," Dirk said. "Herb, would you take Joni and Jeff home?"

"And join us for dinner?" Joni added.

"With pleasure." Gallantly, the older man offered his arm. "Then I will trounce this young hotshot at one of those video games."

"The heck you will!" Jeff cried, clearly looking forward to the prospect of defeating his great-grandfather.

Dirk's eyes met Joni's over the boy's head. The tenderness she saw there reminded her of what had happened the night before. And, even more forcefully, of what he hadn't allowed to happen.

She suspected Dirk planned to stay out late deliberately to avoid a repeat. Well, he needn't worry. He'd made the limits clear, and she intended to honor them.

ON TUESDAY MORNING, Joni returned to work with a sense of relief. The familiar smell of antiseptic at the hospital, the crackle of the intercom and the blandness of the decor helped restore her equilibrium.

Dirk hadn't found any trace of Kim DeLong yesterday. The woman's unexplained absence added yet another puzzle and made Joni long even more for her normal, predictable routine.

"What do you plan to put in next month's employee newsletter?" Basil asked, emerging from his office just as she reached her desk. It apparently never occurred to him to inquire after her health; social graces were not his strong point. "We're behind schedule."

Joni didn't mind her boss's gruff manner. At least, here in the office, she felt safe. "I'll have a list of ideas on your desk by lunchtime." She hoped the staff members had e-mailed her some suggestions while she was gone. In the last newsletter, she'd urged them to do so.

"Also, we need to plan the Christmas party," her boss went on. The public relations team, which consisted of the two of them plus a part-time secretary who was off duty today, was responsible for organizing the affair.

Because nurses, orderlies, technicians and doctors worked around the clock, the party had to overlap two shifts. A small budget made the planning especially tricky.

"I think we should concentrate our efforts this year," she said. "One special tree instead of a lot of cheap decorations. Also, let's skip the party favors and put the money into hiring an outside caterer."

"Food Services will be insulted!"

"Food Services deserves a holiday break too, don't they?" she countered.

"I'll consider it," Basil said, and trudged away. The time change and the early darkness were making him even gloomier than usual, she noted.

Joni sat down to check her e-mail and found, as she'd hoped, a long queue. Food Services proposed on article on how to avoid going overboard on holiday calories; she made a note to follow up on it.

One of the custodians suggested a profile of his dog, Patches, which had placed third in a Frisbee-catching contest. Joni set that one aside, to use only if she were desperate.

She pulled together the best suggestions and printed them out, then opened her accumulated mail and inter-office envelopes. After that, she went over a press release Basil had left for her to expand and edit concerning the acquisition of new imaging equipment.

It lacked details, which she would need to research herself. He'd indicated the press release should go out today, and when Joni checked her watch, she was surprised to see it was already midmorning.

She spent the next hour in the radiology department, learning the ins and outs of the new equipment. Finally, she had enough details and quotes to round out a feature-style release.

At lunchtime, she returned to the office, grabbed her brown bag and headed for the cafeteria. The route took her by the temporary dialysis unit, which had been re-located while the hospital's renal center in a separate building was being remodeled.

As she passed it, two women emerged. One, a heavy-set, elderly woman, was Edith Owens, Fred's mother. She had suffered kidney failure the previous year as a result of diabetes.

The other was Mrs. Wright.

The housekeeper's mouth dropped open at the sight of Joni, then snapped shut. She brushed past, making no attempt to explain. Not that there could be much doubt what she was doing there. No wonder the woman disappeared for hours at a time! She must be undergoing dialysis several times a week.

Joni wanted to reassure her that the Petersons would never penalize her for a health problem. But perhaps pride, or an intense desire for privacy, explained her reaction rather than concern about her job.

"Goodness," Edith said, staring after Mrs. Wright's rapidly departing back. "I wonder what got into her."

"I don't think she wanted me to know about her...condition," Joni said.

"It's nothing to be ashamed of!" Bobby's grandmother said. Joni frequently ran into her at Fred and Kathryn's home; the woman had become close to her daughter-in-law. "Dialysis may be an inconvenience, but it keeps us alive."

"I guess everybody takes it differently." Joni smiled. "I'm on my way to lunch. Care to join me?"

The older woman sighed. "I have to be so careful about what I eat and drink these days that it's easier to dine at home. But thanks for the invitation."

The cafeteria was a dark, low-ceilinged room with an uninspired selection of food. Not recognizing anyone among the diners, Joni bought some soup and a carton of milk, then sat at a table by herself.

So Mrs. Wright had to undergo kidney dialysis. If only she'd felt comfortable confiding in her employer, so much unpleasantness could have been avoided.

Troubled, Joni didn't pay much attention as she finished her soup and pulled her sandwich from its bag. Then something tickled her hand.

She glanced down. A couple of strands of purple and orange were dangling from atop the sandwich bag. For several confused moments, she tried to figure out how they'd gotten there. Jeff often left toys, rocks and other miscellany lying around. Could these bits of fringe have stuck to the sandwich bag by accident?

Purple and orange. The detective had taken Kim's pom-pom pin as evidence; there'd been no fringe left, as far as Joni knew.

She'd left her lunch sack unattended in her office for about an hour this morning. Someone must have entered and placed the strands inside.

If she was right, the stalker had been in the hospital. He had walked into her office. He had touched her lunch.

Her first impulse was to throw the thing in the trash, but she stopped herself. Detective MacDougall might not find this any more convincing than the pom-pom at her house, but perhaps she ought to report it.

Still debating what to do, she dropped the sandwich into the sack. On her way back to the public relations department, she found herself studying everyone she passed, wondering which of them might have done this.

On the threshold of her office, Joni experienced a profound uneasiness. What if the killer had come back while she was gone? Was she going to find some other indication of his presence?

Then she saw the message blinking on her computer screen, indicating an e-mail. That reminded her that she'd forgotten to log off when she left for radiology; but then, she'd never had reason to worry about anyone invading her space.

With a heavy feeling, Joni approached the computer and clicked on the e-mail. Onto the screen flashed a message: "Kick that jerk out of your house or the same thing will happen to him that happened to his brother. I'll be watching."

She stared at it numbly. Who had done this? Why couldn't he leave her alone?

Something Dirk had said came back to her, about the killer wanting to possess her. And to punish her for becoming friendly with Lowell. Was that what this beast was doing—punishing her for letting Dirk move in?

Forcing down her alarm, she checked the tag line and time. The e-mail bore the name Peters and had been sent an hour ago, which meant it had arrived while she was in radiology.

Bernice Peters was the secretary to the hospital's finance director. Fumbling for the phone, Joni dialed her extension.

"Finance director's office."

"Bernice? This is Joni Peterson."

"Hi! Welcome back!"

"Listen, I got a strange e-mail that was sent from your terminal," she said. "Did you see anyone lurking around your office an hour ago?"

"No, Mr. Drummond and I were both in a meeting with the administrator," the secretary said. "Oh, my gosh, I didn't think to log off. It's never been a problem."

The finance office was situated along the hospital's main corridor, with a stream of patients, staff and visitors going by. Easily accessible, although also easily observed. The killer had taken quite a chance. He must have a good excuse for being in the hospital and figured he could bluff his way out if questioned.

Mrs. Wright came to mind. She'd been there, but the scenario didn't fit with Joni's impression of the older woman.

Kim DeLong served on the hospital's governing board; her father had been one of the institution's original investors. Under normal circumstances, she could easily have done this. But she'd been missing since Saturday.

The perpetrator was probably too smart to have left fingerprints in Bernice's office, but Joni had to report this. She didn't realize how deeply she'd been disturbed until she picked up the phone to call the police and saw her hands were trembling.

DIRK COULD HARDLY SIT still all day Tuesday. A restlessness nagged at him as he placed one phone call after another to his associates abroad; pounded on the computer keyboard; prowled through the printing company's offices.

He needed answers. And he needed relief from his own turmoil.

His old foe, self-doubt, whispered that he was failing Joni. That he wasn't smart enough or quick enough to save her from this darkness closing in around them. That he had barely been strong enough to rein in his own desires.

On Sunday, when they fell into each other's arms, he'd wanted to take her ten different ways. To open himself to her, demand more of her than she'd ever given before and let the fire consume them both.

It was more than physical desire. He'd kept aloof from any real attachment for so long that he hadn't realized how much he ached for intimacy. Returning to Viento del Mar had unleashed a lot of demons: along with self-doubt, an aching need to belong to someone, a wild passion that impeded rational thought.

This time, however, there was a real demon. A killer who possessed an uncanny ability to counter their movements and to prowl freely, unobserved. To taunt them.

Dirk's searches on the Internet yielded frustratingly inconclusive tidbits. Celia Lu's husband had been investigated on suspicion of smuggling Chinese artifacts, but these consisted of so few items that they were most likely personal possessions not intended for sale. Customs authorities had declined to prosecute.

Three years earlier, Basil Dupont had been convicted of drunken driving but had remained clean ever since. As for the soccer coach, even this small town had four residents named Charles Rogers, two of whom lived in the same apartment building. Dirk left a message at the soccer league's office requesting the man's driver's license number. Since most of the league officials knew the Peterson family, he hoped they would cooperate.

Kim DeLong hadn't used her credit card since Friday. None of her old friends would admit to having heard from her, either.

By lunchtime, Dirk began to wonder if he were coming down with a fever. His body felt hot, on the edge of exploding.

He took a walk to burn off energy. After a few blocks, he passed the hospital and wondered how Joni was feeling. But he didn't want to disturb her at work.

At the intersection of Canyon Vista and San Bernardo roads stood a real-estate company. Impulsively, Dirk went inside and talked to a Realtor about selling the Peterson mansion, noting that he preferred a buyer who would retain the present staff. The man promised to draw up paperwork for a listing.

The prospect of putting the house on the market gave Dirk a small sense of relief. That and the walk helped dispel his tension, and that afternoon he was able to focus on the material his brother had left regarding the new publishing venture.

Lowell had acquired one manuscript already. Wondering whether Joni might enjoy editing it, Dirk thumbed through the typed pages. *The Post-Millennial Boom: Beyond the Internet,* written by an Australian computer whiz, speculated about evolving technologies that would revolutionize international business dealings. Dirk found it fascinating.

By the time he finished, several hours had passed. His mind hummed with possibilities, both for marketing this book and for commissioning others. This line could be sold around the world via the Internet from a base right here in Viento del Mar.

But he couldn't stay. The town was too confining and too full of ghosts from Dirk's past for him ever to live there again.

On the drive home, he saw that the cloud cover had thinned, permitting a streaky pink sunset. However, the radio forecast called for rain later in the week. By prior arrangement, he picked up a pizza. Finding himself the first one home, he changed out of his suit and sat down to watch the business news on PBS.

"The market apparently got the pre-Halloween jitters today," the announcer began. "It was definitely a trick rather than a treat for investors…"

Thursday would be Halloween, Dirk recalled. It was also Joni's thirtieth birthday. What kind of gift could he give her? Something special, but not excessive. Something brother-in-lawish, he thought with a trace of irony.

Into his mind popped an image of the velvet jewelry box his brother had given Kim. Diamond earrings hardly seemed appropriate under the circumstances, however. A gold watch? Too impersonal. A hair ornament? Too ordinary, he mused.

The perfect gift lay just out of reach in the back of

his mind, taunting him. Well, he would figure it out by Thursday, Dirk told himself.

The *whir* of the garage door announced Jeff and Joni's arrival. As soon as he saw her pale, drawn face, he knew something was wrong.

"I'm just tired," Joni responded to his questions, but he sensed she didn't want to talk in front of the boy. "I'm going to rest."

"I'll bring you dinner on a tray later," he said.

Unaware of the undercurrents, Jeff chattered as he ate. His P.E. instructor, he informed Dirk, had tested the third graders for fitness, and he'd been the second fastest runner in his class.

"Good for you!"

The little boy let out a long breath. "I wish I could tell Dad."

He touched the little boy's hand. "Wherever he is, I'll bet he's proud of you."

Jeff smiled, but he didn't look convinced.

Afterward, Dirk helped him go over his math homework. Jeff had a quick mind but tended to be careless; once he added where he should have subtracted and he forgot to carry a number while multiplying.

"Accuracy is vital," Dirk said. "Suppose NASA miscalculated and they sent a rocket to Jupiter instead of Mars? They might run out of fuel."

"They should carry extra gas just in case," Jeff proposed.

"It would be easier to do the math right in the first place."

The little boy wrinkled his nose. "Yeah, okay."

Being able to help his son, even for that little bit, gave Dirk a sense of satisfaction. Long after Jeff went to bed, it continued to warm him.

He cleaned up the kitchen and then checked on his son. Jeff had fallen asleep with *Charlotte's Web* propped on his chest. Smiling, Dirk set the book aside and switched off the lamp. He lingered there, drinking in the peaceful sight of the little boy sleeping.

When he withdrew, he saw that the door to Joni's room stood ajar. Inside, a light was on. It was time to keep his promise of bringing her dinner.

In a kitchen cabinet, he found a wooden tray with snap-open legs. Dirk reheated some pizza, added a few sprigs of parsley to dress it up and poured a glass of mineral water. He would've liked to complete the picture with a rosebud but didn't want to stumble around outside in the dark trying to pick one.

Humming, he carried the tray through the house. Without a free hand, he couldn't knock, but he bumped the door a couple of times with his knee. When Joni didn't answer, he shouldered it open and went in.

The bedroom was empty, but the door to the master bath stood ajar. "Joni?" he called. "I've brought dinner."

"In here!" Her voice had a refreshing lilt. "It's okay. I'm decent."

Curious, Dirk edged inside with the tray. The room was larger than he'd expected, with a spa set into an alcove beneath a rippled window.

Amid a light froth of bubbles, Joni reclined in the water. She wore a Hawaiian-print swimsuit, ruffled at the bust and clinging to her slender midriff. Blond hair wisped from its knot atop her head, creating a halo around her face. In the rising steam, her skin appeared creamy and moist.

Dirk could feel his muscles tightening. Getting a grip on himself, he set the tray on the edge of the spa.

"I'm glad to see you're relaxing." He couldn't resist adding, "Do you always wear a swimsuit in the tub?"

"No, but it occurred to me, with all that's been going on, I should be prepared to get out in a hurry." Her mouth twisted wryly. "Anyway, this looks terrific. Thank you."

Dirk sat on the edge of the spa. He knew it would be prudent to leave, but they needed to talk. "You were upset about something earlier."

She finished a bite of pizza. "At work, I got an e-mail threatening your life if you don't move out. I tried to call you, but you were out and you must have had your cell phone switched off."

"The battery died," he said. "I didn't realize it until later." He'd found a replacement in Lowell's desk.

It shouldn't surprise him that the stalker knew he was living here, but the confirmation disturbed Dirk. While they were fruitlessly sorting through clues, this man had been watching them.

"Did you call MacDougall?"

"Yes, but the computer it came from had been left unattended, and there weren't any suspicious fingerprints."

"It was interoffice? The message was sent from within the hospital?"

She nodded grimly. "There's more. Whoever did it came into my office while I was in another part of the building. He—or she—left a couple of strands from a pom-pom in my lunch bag. I gave those to the police, too."

Mentally, Dirk turned over this information. The fact that the stalker had physically invaded Joni's workplace was disturbing.

Could it be a co-worker? A patient? "You didn't notice anyone in the building who seemed out of place?"

She frowned. "I did see Mrs. Wright. It turns out she's a dialysis patient. That must be where she's been going several times a week."

No wonder the housekeeper had been so touchy. With her reticent nature, she'd resented even innocent questions about her whereabouts.

"I hope she's all right," Dirk said. "You don't think she's responsible for the e-mail, do you?"

"I checked, and she was hooked up to a machine at the time it was sent," Joni said. "Kim could have written it, but she's still missing. Besides, I keep getting the feeling it's a man."

"Why? Because of the footprint in the blind?"

"And that comment you made about the killer trying to punish me for making friends with Lowell. That sounds like a jealous man." Without warning, a tear slipped down her cheek.

Reaching out with the tip of his thumb, Dirk gently wiped away the drop. "What is it?"

"I wish I'd given Lowell the benefit of the doubt," she said miserably. "He was trying to protect me, and I accused him of being the stalker."

"I can't blame you, not when he'd done the same thing before. The tragedy is that he died just as he was learning some important lessons."

Dirk wished, more than ever, that he'd had a chance to talk to his brother one more time, heart to heart. To know him as the human being he'd finally become.

"I should've seen that he'd changed."

"You're the one who made him grow up," Dirk said. "He was lucky he found you, and in the end I think he was smart enough to realize it."

The expression on her face was so wistful that, without stopping to consider, he leaned forward and brushed his lips across hers. When he drew back, her gaze smoldered at him.

"Do that again," she said.

"I'm not sure we should—"

One slim, wet arm reached out and pulled him forward. When his mouth met hers, Dirk lost track of where he was, of everything but the increasing pressure of their lips.

His tongue traced her teeth and probed deeper. A sudden intake of breath told him she was responding with an intensity that matched his own.

When she came up for air, Joni said, "Take your shirt off."

"Why?"

She gave a low chuckle. "Because I'm dripping all over you."

He felt a surge of recklessness. "I like wet clothes." Without stopping to consider, he slid into the tub beside her, blue jeans, polo shirt, socks and all.

It was a strange feeling, squishy and naughty. Joni's laughter tickled across his nerve endings. "I can't believe you did that!"

"Neither can I." Dirk started to laugh, too. Beneath his good humor, however, he could feel himself responding to Joni's half-naked presence. Eve must have been like this, he thought. Ripe and tempting, and scarcely aware of it.

He knew he ought to drag himself away while he still could. Then he realized that he couldn't. Maybe he was selfish, or maybe crazy, but an exquisite hunger raged inside him that only Joni could satisfy.

"I thought I was modest, but this is ridiculous," she teased. "Taking a bath with your clothes on!"

"As long as it doesn't get in the way," he said, and gathered her in his arms.

In the water, she seemed to float onto his lap. Her legs tangled with his, and suddenly Dirk could no longer bear the confinement of clothes separating them.

Chapter Twelve

Joni's self-consciousness yielded to a languorous delight. Being held by Dirk, so close and yet protected by their clothing, allowed her to luxuriate in the sensations tingling through her body.

The barriers between them blurred. Even through the fabric, she could feel his reactions almost as if they were hers.

His hard muscles made her keenly aware of her own softness. Of the fiery need to be touched, on her face and breasts and hips. To be filled by him.

Curling against Dirk, Joni inhaled his musky fragrance, enhanced by the effect of water. When his mouth sought hers again, she danced her tongue along the edge of his lips, relishing the way his grip tightened around her.

She had never before experienced this combination of desire and comfort, of complete trust. If only it could last forever, the passion rising but never requiring fulfillment. Perhaps, tonight, anything was possible.

As Dirk explored her mouth, his hand slipped the strap from her shoulder. Warm water caressed her bare breast, and his mouth followed. Once, in some other life, she had felt clumsy and boyish. Now, beneath his kisses, her natural voluptuousness blossomed.

When he caught the erect nipple, a profound yearning lashed Joni. Her breasts swelled with desire as he slid down her other strap.

Avidly, she feathered her hands across Dirk's shoulders, prizing their sculpted firmness. She wanted to touch him freely, to cherish his masculine beauty, to be some wild, sensual creature with no fear of consequences.

Hungrily, she helped him pull the wet shirt upward. As he lifted it over his head, she angled forward and brushed her nipples across his bronzed skin.

With a moan, Dirk caught her hips to his. His masculine hardness indented her, a warning and a promise.

Joni wanted this moment, this treasure. No other reality existed.

Dirk's breathing rasped as she unsnapped his soaked, clinging jeans and lowered the zipper. The other night, he had stopped her at this point. This time, the prospect would be unendurable.

She tugged the denim down his thighs. He was hard, all right, but acquiescent, leaning back in the tub so she could wrest the jeans free.

As she tossed them aside, powerful hands caught her swimsuit and worked it down her rib cage. Stripping her, Dirk found the sensitive inlets of her waist and navel, then the crease between her thighs.

Joni craved everything at once, all of him touching all of her. Yet she remained kneeling, motionless, as he found her most sensitive point and stroked it.

"Dirk," she whispered. "I want…"

"I know." His voice vibrated close to her ear.

He knelt before her in the water, and now they *were*

in contact at every point. Merging seamlessly, yet still not one.

His hands caught her derriere and lifted her. For one moment, Joni felt weightless and suspended before he shifted her against his groin and eased himself inside her. His vibrant masculinity extended her. A joy as pure as flame shot through Joni.

His movements began slowly, subtly, and then the rhythm intensified. She augmented his fluid music with a seductive counterpoint that spurred him on until his eyes narrowed in pleasure.

As his mouth probed hers, his movements speeded into an erotic dance. Why had she never realized she was capable of such sweet sensations?

Tightly, she pressed into Dirk, teasing and summoning him. He rocketed into her, lifting her, thrilling her. Passion exploded into ecstasy as the last shreds of control burst.

Joni soared with him, scarcely aware of the water around them. The world filled with colored lights, playing across her skin and glowing within her.

A wave of pure satisfaction made her so buoyant that Joni clutched his shoulders to anchor herself. She had the impression that they hovered above the pool, snatched from ordinary time and space into a realm of their own.

At last they subsided together, spent but luminous. She nestled against Dirk, not wanting to talk, just to feel his rapid breathing and know that he, too, had experienced something special.

It occurred to her, too late, that they should have been more careful. She'd already had one child by this man; she knew he was potent. But then, with a twinge that might almost be disappointment, she realized it was the wrong time of the month.

It didn't matter. The experience they had just shared was something she would always treasure no matter how empty the future might be.

DIRK STRUGGLED to understand this mad joy soaring through him. What had happened between him and Joni had elevated him to a new level of awareness.

The physical pleasure might be extreme, but even stronger was the profound sense of connection. They had forged a link whose implications he couldn't yet grasp.

Still, he couldn't afford to indulge in romanticism. The world would not stay on hold. In fact, he suspected that reality was due for a crash landing any minute.

Slowly Dirk drew into himself. When he did, he realized he was sitting in a tub of cooling water, with his wet clothes slopped onto the floor and Joni half-asleep against his shoulder.

From experience, he knew all too well how easily what began with loving spontaneity could end with disappointment and bitterness. He should have been more careful. He should have controlled himself.

"Time for bed," he murmured. She nodded vaguely.

As he helped her dry off, Dirk hoped that what had happened wouldn't damage their friendship. How could he have risked their closeness by yielding to impulse no matter how much gratification it gave him? Jeff needed them both, as parents, not as lovers in a volatile relationship.

After tucking Joni under the covers, he wrung out his clothes, wrapped himself in a towel and carried the wet garments to the utility room. Then he returned to the master bedroom.

It might be more prudent to spend the rest of the night in the sofa bed, but he couldn't bear to leave that much space between them. As he lay down beside Joni, her warmth flooded him, bringing back tingling memories.

Tomorrow, he would find a way to persuade her that they must go back to behaving as they had before. To being merely friends, for their son's sake.

BY THE TIME JONI AWAKENED on Wednesday morning, Dirk had left the room, but she could tell he'd slept there. The spare pillow retained a trace of his aftershave lotion, and there was an indentation where he'd lain. She wished he hadn't gone. But, for Jeff's sake, they needed to be discreet.

Not only for Jeff. What if the stalker realized they were sleeping together?

A chill crept down her spine. Could someone have been watching the house last night? She kept the blinds closed, but the stalker appeared to be both bold and intuitive.

If he suspected anything, she had no doubt there would be repercussions. Joni's throat clenched as she pictured someone attacking Dirk. He needed to be careful, and so did she.

She dressed and went out. Jeff was still asleep. In the utility room, she found Dirk removing his jeans from the dryer. He looked starchily remote in a business suit.

"Hello," she said.

When he glanced up, his face had an opaque tightness. "Good morning."

"I've been thinking," she said.

"So have I."

She pressed on. "It's about the killer. If he suspects

what happened between us last night, he might act to-day."

Dirk straightened. He looked ill at ease in the cramped room. "There are a lot of reasons why we need to be cautious," he said quietly. "Last night—I don't want to call it a mistake, but we were careless."

"I don't think I'm pregnant," she said. "Wrong timing."

From his startled look, she gathered that hadn't been what he meant. "I never...well, that's fortunate. Because even though you mean a great deal to me, I don't want to raise false expectations."

Expectations? Certainly she didn't expect Dirk to change his life to suit her, but she had hoped for something more than this studied coolness. "Do you want to pretend it didn't happen?"

"We can hardly do that." Warmth flickered in his eyes. "My first concern is for your safety, yours and Jeff's. MacDougall already believes I lack objectivity. We don't want to give him any further reason to discredit whatever clues we turn up. For that and other reasons, we need to back off."

A tight band of disappointment squeezed her chest, but she supposed he was right. "They're installing the alarm system this afternoon. You could move out if you think it's necessary."

"There's no need to make a decision yet," he said. "Right now, I want to get an early start at the office. I keep feeling there's some detail eluding me. Something I should be able to find in the computer or in Lowell's papers."

Joni made a quick mental review of her plans for the day. She would be leaving her job early to let the workmen into the house and then she would pick up her son for soccer practice.

Kathryn had offered to take him since she got off early from her shift as a supermarket cashier. But Jeff needed as much support as possible right now, and Joni wanted to be with him.

"Jeff has soccer practice at four, in Del Mar Park," she said. "You're welcome to join us."

"I'll try." He gave her a distracted half smile. "Don't ever think that last night didn't mean a great deal to me, because it did."

"Me, too," she said, but when they tried to hug each other goodbye, they seemed to have too many arms and noses.

After Dirk left, Joni awakened her son and fixed breakfast. Unsettled emotions flickered through her, embryonic happiness dampened by an incipient sense of dread.

She was mature enough to understand that not every fierce attraction could grow into a long-lasting love. Dirk cared about her, but last night might remain forever a unique and isolated memory.

It had been worth it.

As usual, Dirk checked his car before getting in. There were no signs of tampering.

Criminals generally stuck to one method of dispatching their victims, and the stalker had shown a preference for knives. That didn't mean, however, that he might not be clever enough to employ whatever weapon suited his purpose.

Today, more than ever, Dirk ached to watch over Joni. But if danger threatened, it was more likely to target him. At least, he hoped so.

He checked the rearview mirror more often than usual in case he was being followed. Even the slightest anomaly, such as the rattle of a truck hitting a pothole or an odor that took a moment to identify as eau de skunk, set his adrenaline pumping.

Halloween witches and skeletons adorned the neighborhood windows along the way, some of them startlingly realistic. Beside the road, a figure swung from a tree. Dirk's grip tightened on the steering wheel until he registered the shape as a life-size scarecrow.

Still on edge, he turned into the parking lot of Peterson Printing. The copy shop in front wouldn't open for several hours, and he cut through an empty lot toward the main plant. Near a side entrance clustered a dozen cars belonging to night-shift workers. Beyond them, delivery trucks waited beside the closed loading dock.

Dirk's reserved space was located around back, next to the administrative offices. He would almost certainly be the first to arrive. He steered toward his space, then braked abruptly. Something dark lay crumpled in the middle of it.

It flashed into his mind that someone had dumped trash on the pavement. Then, as he stared at the shape, he remembered the scarecrow in the tree. But this sprawled, plastic-shrouded figure looked too solid to be stuffed with rags.

Dirk backed up and cut off the engine. The lot was secluded, with a small industrial park on one side and a warehouse on the other, although he could hear the swish of traffic from San Bernardo Road.

Holding his cellular phone in one hand, he got out and walked toward the parking space. He kept hoping his impression would prove wrong.

A few more steps, and he made out the contours of a

human figure draped in a plastic sheet. Long dark hair pooled like blood around the head.

His gut clenching, Dirk dialed 911.

JONI HAD DROPPED JEFF at school and was en route to the hospital when she glimpsed flashing lights and police cars at the printing company.

Dirk. What if he'd been attacked?

Without hesitation, she spun into the lot. She couldn't bear to lose him, not this way, not now.

An ambulance jounced by her, going in the other direction. No lights, no siren. Either it was empty or the person inside must be dead.

A glaze came over her eyes. It took all Joni's presence of mind to steer through the maze of parked emergency vehicles toward the administrative office in back.

As she rounded the building, she recognized the lank form of Detective MacDougall, standing to one side, wearing what appeared to be the same rumpled jacket as always. He was talking to a tall man in a business suit who faced away from Joni.

She knew those broad shoulders, that short dark hair. Relief tingled through her, but her hands still felt slippery on the wheel.

Dirk was safe. What had happened, then, to bring out half the town's police force?

Leaving the car in the first available space, Joni hurried over. MacDougall spotted her first, and Dirk pivoted.

"What's going on?" To her surprise, she was nearly breathless. "I was going to work and I saw all the patrol cars."

"Come with me." The detective moved her away

from Dirk and out of earshot. "Where were you last night?"

"At home." She regarded him quizzically.

"Where was Mr. Peterson?"

"At my house, too."

"All night?" When she nodded, the detective pressed, "Can you swear to that? Was he in the same room with you? Don't look at Mr. Peterson! I want your honest answer."

Joni sighed. There was no sense in denying it. "Yes, he was in the same room with me. Now what's happened?"

Apparently, she'd given the right answer, the one that matched Dirk's, because the detective's expression eased. "I'm afraid your brother-in-law has found the body of Mrs. DeLong."

"What?" This made no sense. Joni had believed the stalker was after her or those close to her. "Why would anyone kill Kim?"

"Maybe they had reason to hold a grudge."

"You mean me?" Her hand flew to her throat. "You think *I* killed her?"

Dirk strode toward them. "Give her a break, MacDougall. She had nothing to do with this."

The detective blocked his path. "I need to talk to Mrs. Peterson alone."

Above MacDougall's outstretched arm, deep blue eyes met hers. "You should have a lawyer present, Joni."

"I have nothing to hide." She knew she sounded naive. But waiting for a lawyer would only drag this matter out and reinforce the policeman's suspicion of her.

"This way, please." The detective gestured her toward the building.

In a private office, he questioned her for nearly an hour, taking particular note that both Celia and Dirk could attest to her whereabouts on Saturday night. She held nothing back, knowing he must have interrogated Dirk and that their answers would be compared.

When he was finished, he grudgingly answered a few questions of her own, probably because the information would soon be all over the media anyway. It appeared that Kim DeLong had been stabbed to death several days ago, possibly on Saturday night.

"The blood," Joni said, "on my patio. Could the killer have dumped it there?"

"Since it was washed off, we have no way of knowing who it belonged to." MacDougall's pouchy face looked gray, as if he were upset over the gruesome find, too.

"I'm sorry," she said. "Kim did some rotten things, but she didn't deserve this."

"I'm releasing you for now." The detective inhaled as if intending to say more, then stood up and opened the door. "I may have more questions later."

"I understand," Joni said.

Outside, investigators were taking measurements and bagging evidence. Yellow tape encircled the rear of the building, and arriving employees had to use the side door.

Dirk stood near the secured area, watching the activity. When he caught sight of Joni, he started toward her, until the detective waved him away. Reluctantly, Joni got into her car. She wanted to stick this out, but she was late for work.

Although the alarm system would be installed at her home this afternoon, that prospect no longer reassured her. Kim's elegant Tudor mansion, adjacent to the country club, bore a sign proclaiming the name of her security service. What good had it done?

Trying to keep her thoughts trained on the day ahead, Joni drove to the hospital beneath low, ominous clouds.

THE DETECTIVE KEPT ASKING for the same information, trying to trip him up. After laboriously repeating his description of where he had been Saturday night and how he had found the body this morning, Dirk got annoyed.

"Look," he said, "Joni's in danger. Why are you more interested in trying to pin this on me than in protecting her?"

The detective tilted his jowly head. "What I'd like to know, Mr. Peterson, is why you aren't more concerned about your own safety. Do you have some inside information about where this guy's going to strike next?"

"I'm not the killer," Dirk said. "And I can take care of myself."

"Do you carry a gun?"

"Of course not." California had strict laws against concealed weapons. "Since you've already searched me and impounded my car, you're well aware that I don't."

He supposed it might be more forthright to admit that seeing Kim's body had left him with a chill deep in his gut. But it wouldn't do any good.

MacDougall must have serious doubts about whether Joni, newly released from the hospital, could have confronted Kim, murdered her and dragged the body away. So the detective was taking the easy way out by turning his sights on Dirk.

"We're aware that you don't have a gun on you," the detective conceded. "But then, the victim was stabbed."

If he were trying to get Dirk's goat, he was succeeding. "Let's put our cards on the table," Dirk snapped. "Why would I kill Kim DeLong? Because we had one argument at a soccer field?"

"According to witnesses, you were angry that she'd seduced your brother and embarrassed your family," the detective said mildly. Luring him, giving him an opening to spew out his fury.

Dirk sighed. "I had nothing to gain from her death and you know it. From my brother's, I got a job I didn't need."

"As well as half ownership of his property," the man prompted. "He was fairly wealthy, I gather."

MacDougall was clearly out of his depth. "This may come as a disappointment to you, but in this case, 'wealthy' is a relative term. First of all, in case you haven't already checked, my own net worth far exceeds my brother's. Furthermore, most of his capital is tied up in the printing company, which is still in debt from its expansion."

The detective rubbed his jaw. "The two of you didn't get along, did you?"

"You're fishing in the wrong creek," Dirk said. "Come on, MacDougall. Don't tell me you haven't checked my whereabouts last Wednesday night. I wasn't even in Viento del Mar."

He could see resistance in the man's face. The detective sure hated to give up an easy solution. "Not as far as we can tell anyway."

"Then I'm free to go?"

"I wouldn't say that."

They'd been over the facts repeatedly. Moreover, they were wasting time. Somewhere nearby, a killer lurked. If MacDougall didn't intend to hunt down the clues, then someone else had to.

"Am I under arrest?" Dirk demanded. "If I am, I want a lawyer. If not, I've got work to do."

The policeman's cheeks twitched as if he were chewing gum. Finally, he said, "Don't leave town without notifying us."

"I have no intention of leaving town until I'm sure Joni and my s—my nephew are safe."

The other man's eyebrows rose. "Your what, Mr. Peterson?"

He'd just slipped, Dirk realized. If the truth came out, it could look very bad indeed.

Chapter Thirteen

Your what, Mr. Peterson? The detective's words echoed in Dirk's ears.

"My son," he answered, since it was obvious that's what he'd started to say. "That's how I've come to think of him. I have no children of my own, as you should know."

"You wouldn't be planning to adopt your nephew, would you?" MacDougall pressed. "Say, once you and Mrs. Peterson get married?"

So that was what the man was implying. If Dirk had been secretly planning to marry Joni and wanted to adopt Jeff, it would give him a motive to get rid of Lowell.

"Until last week, I'd only met my sister-in-law at her wedding and my father's funeral, and I'd never met my nephew," Dirk said. "What's between Joni and me occurred *after* my brother's death. For your information, we haven't discussed marriage."

He stopped short of explaining that he wasn't the type to tie himself to one place. That was none of Mac-Dougall's business.

"I suppose you wouldn't mind if we check Mrs. Peterson's phone records?" the detective said.

"You don't need my permission." Dirk had no doubt

the man would pursue that avenue if he hadn't already done so. "But you won't find any international calls to me. Also, my passport will show that I rarely visit this country."

The other man shrugged. "All right, Mr. Peterson." As Dirk withdrew, he added, "Hey!"

"Yes?"

"I'm real sorry about your printing plant being in debt. Inheriting it must have put a big strain on your finances." MacDougall kept his tone deadpan as he jingled the change in his pocket. "You need a small loan or anything?"

"I'll let you know," Dirk retorted, and headed for the side entrance.

ALL DAY, JONI JUMPED every time the phone rang. Her breath caught in her throat as she read through her e-mail, and she made a point of buying lunch.

No more surprises, please.

At least she didn't risk running into Mrs. Wright. Patients wouldn't normally undergo dialysis two days in a row.

The scene at the printing plant kept running through her mind: police cruisers and a fire truck parked helter-skelter; yellow tape blocking the crime scene; investigators poring over every pebble and fallen leaf.

Kim's body had already been removed, and Joni was glad she hadn't seen it. But a sense of horror remained, mixed with troubling questions. Why had the killer targeted Kim? Did he have the twisted notion that he was avenging her wrongs to Joni, or did he fear Kim might have information about Lowell's death? Or was there yet another, unsuspected motive?

She shivered at the possibility that Kim's blood had

been dumped on her patio after the murder. What about the pom-pom pin left at the house on Sunday? And the strands found in her lunch sack yesterday?

The killer was close to her. Much too close.

Did he really fantasize about winning Joni and then keeping her under his thumb? The very idea gave her the creeps.

Once she told Basil what had happened at Dirk's plant, he forgave her lateness, but he reminded her that the newsletter needed to go out. She set to work determined to make the best use of the few hours available.

Her boss helped by steering away a newspaper reporter who wanted to interview her. From the hallway, she could hear his gravelly voice explaining that Mrs. Peterson was too upset to talk.

The young woman apologized and left. Whether Herb had spoken to his friend, the publisher, or whether the reporter was simply respecting small-town sensibilities, Joni was grateful that she apparently wouldn't be harassed.

At one o'clock, as she drove home to meet the security service, the radio announcer was recounting the news of Kim's death.

"Police are withholding information about where Mrs. DeLong's body might have been hidden since Saturday," he intoned. "However, this station has learned that twigs and leaves were clinging to the plastic sheet found wrapped around her. This might indicate the hiding place was in a wooded area."

There were plenty of woods around Viento del Mar, Joni reminded herself. It didn't mean Kim's body had been kept near her house.

"There were no signs of forced entry at Mrs. De-Long's home," the man continued. "She was believed to have been alone Saturday night, and some observers speculate she might have opened the door to someone she knew.

"Mrs. DeLong was known to have argued earlier in the day with Joni Peterson, ex-wife of businessman, Lowell Peterson, and with Peterson's brother, Dirk. Lowell Peterson was stabbed to death one week ago—"

Joni switched off the radio. How dare the newscaster imply there was a connection between the argument and Kim's slaying?

It was also unreasonable for anyone to assume that a woman would only open the door to an acquaintance. Viento del Mar was a small town with a low crime rate. Lots of people opened their doors for salesmen, Mormon missionaries, and stranded motorists.

There was no mention of the police having found a murder weapon. She wondered whether the killer had used the same kind of knife and where it was now.

DIRK SPENT MUCH of the day reassuring employees about the murder, answering questions for the police and dodging a reporter and photographer who were hanging around the crime scene. He also had to arrange for another rental car, since his had been impounded pending a search.

In the little free time that remained, he checked the computer for anything in Kim's background that might provide a lead. Her ex-husband. Her financial situation. Her charitable activities.

If the information existed, it wasn't in her credit files or anywhere else that he could access. Although he wanted very much to interview the victim's friends, Dirk suspected MacDougall would arrest him for interfering with a police investigation if he tried.

At three-thirty, Joni called to say the alarm system had been installed and she was going to collect Jeff for soccer practice. Dirk was relieved to hear her voice.

He wanted to talk about last night, about the need to maintain their friendship for Jeff's sake, but he preferred not to risk being overheard. Mostly he wanted to drive to her house and corner her in the bedroom, free her hair from its knot and remove both their clothes.

Exactly what he must not allow himself to do. Not now, and maybe never again.

"I'll try to make it to soccer practice," he told her, "but there's a news team outside. I don't want to risk having them follow me to the park and disrupt everything."

"I don't think they would, but we can't be sure," she said. "See you later, then."

After she hung up, Dirk sat at his desk, thinking about her. He missed the softness of her hair, the glow in her eyes and the silky vibrancy of her skin. He wanted an instant replay of last night.

But he could feel the past and the town itself closing around him like a vise. The expectations, speculations and intrusions left him no privacy. Now he couldn't even go for a walk without being pestered.

The world outside his hometown, Dirk had discovered long ago, was a wonderful place to hide. He loved the thrill of entering an unfamiliar country and meeting the unknown head-on.

After growing up in such a claustrophobic environment, he enjoyed the anonymity of strolling down a street where no one knew his name or expected anything from him. To be seen exclusively for oneself meant freedom.

Oddly, he didn't get the lift that usually accompanied

his musings about travel. His mind kept returning to one small house, to one intriguing woman—

"Dirk?"

He looked up. His grandfather stood in the doorway. "Herb! Good to see you!"

The older man, as straight and confident as ever, returned the greeting. As he took a seat, however, Dirk could see the tension in his face. "I heard about Kim on the radio."

"I'm still in shock," Dirk admitted. "Even my experiences as a bodyguard didn't prepare me for finding the body of someone I've known for years."

"How's Joni taking it?"

"She had an alarm system installed and now she's on her way to soccer practice," he said. "She's trying to keep things normal for Jeff."

"I've been wondering if I should spend more time with them," Herb said. "Not that I'm much of a fighter. But this murderer, he might back off if she's with someone."

"Or it might make him angry," Dirk pointed out.

His grandfather cleared his throat and shifted on the hard chair. "You know, when I asked you to look into Lowell's death, I never meant to put you or anyone else in danger."

"You think my snooping contributed to Kim's getting killed?" Dirk couldn't see a connection, but Herb knew this town better than he did.

"I'm not sure." Thick silver hair stood up as the older man ran his fingers through it. "I've been mulling over this whole business all day, trying to come up with some useful approach."

It might not be Herb's job to solve crimes, but then, it wasn't Dirk's job, either, he mused. The Peterson men responded to life's blows by taking action or trying to, and his grandfather was no exception.

"I don't like them staying in the house where Lowell died," Herb went on. "Since Jeff owns half of the estate anyway, I think they should move there. I will, too. The boy needs masculine guidance."

Dirk wondered how his grandfather would react if he learned the truth about Jeff's paternity, or that Dirk and Joni were having an affair. Most likely, it would only trouble him unnecessarily.

"I suggested they move back, but Joni vetoed it. In fact, I've listed it with a real-estate agent." Dirk glanced at the clock. It was after four; soccer practice should have started.

Herb frowned. "I don't like them living alone in that place after you leave. Alarm or not, I'm surprised Joni can stand it."

"She thinks the stalker will follow her wherever she goes." Dirk hoped his grandfather's worrying wouldn't affect his heart condition. "I'll tell her you've offered to join her at the estate. Maybe that will make a difference. A couple of buyers want to see the property, but I don't expect it to sell right away."

"Thanks." Herb stood and shook hands. "I appreciate everything you've done."

After he left, the secretary buzzed Dirk. "You had a call while you were with Mr. Peterson. It didn't sound important, so I took a message."

"What was it?" Idly, Dirk jotted down a name and a phone number. Liz at the soccer league. Then he remembered that he'd requested information about the coach.

He returned the call immediately. Liz, a pleasant-sounding woman with a no-nonsense manner, told him it was Charlie's second year as a coach and that he worked for a plumbing contractor. He'd said that he'd never been convicted of a crime, but the league hadn't double-checked. If Dirk liked, she would fax over a copy of the application.

He would like it. Very much.

THE PARK'S SOCCER FIELD lacked bleachers, so Joni spread a blanket on the grass next to the Owenses. In the moisture-laden breeze, she could feel the curl evaporating from her hair and hoped she wasn't going to catch a chill through her light jacket.

The other parents kept their distance, but this time she was prepared to be cold-shouldered. Anyway, she preferred it to intrusive questions.

On the field, Charlie shouted encouragement as he put the boys through calisthenics. Although he wore jeans and a pullover, his close-cropped blond hair gave him a military air.

"I hope it's not going to rain tomorrow night," Kathryn said. "Not after all the work I put into those costumes."

"The kids could go to the Halloween party at church," Fred suggested. "That will be indoors."

"It's not the same as trick-or-treating, but I suppose they'd have to," his wife said. "What do you think, Joni?"

At the prompting, Joni gave voice to a nagging worry. "I've been concerned about letting Jeff go door-to-door this year, with a murderer loose in Viento del Mar. The church sounds like a good idea."

"I guess you're right," Kathryn said. "That was just horrible about Mrs. DeLong."

Her husband touched her arm warningly. "Maybe we should talk about something else."

"Oh! That reminds me," Kathryn told Joni. "I was going to suggest that Jeff come home with us tonight. That way, if you want to watch a newscast or if the police come by with questions, he won't have to see it. I know this whole situation's been tough on him."

The boy *would* enjoy staying overnight with Bobby. More than that, it would give Joni a chance to talk privately with Dirk.

"That's a wonderful idea," she said. "I don't know what I'd do without you two."

"Don't thank us," said Fred. "Bobby's a lot less trouble when he has company. The two of them sit in front of the computer and we don't hear a peep out of them."

The boys began kicking the ball across the grass, each vying to get a whack at it. The Owenses' attention shifted away, and of their own accord, Joni's thoughts flew to Dirk.

She wished she knew how he felt about the change in their relationship last night. This morning, he'd seemed withdrawn.

Was he afraid she would try to cling to him? If so, she would soon disabuse him of that notion.

Joni had learned from her mother's experience that a woman needed to stand on her own two feet. All she wanted from Dirk was whatever part of himself he could give freely. If he wished, they could go back to being— what? Casual friends who shared only their affection for Jeff?

Anguish twisted inside her. She couldn't imagine never again enjoying the throbbing, tingling, steaming excitement they had discovered last night. She wanted to see those piercing blue eyes every morning, to meet him in the kitchen every evening and exchange impressions of the day.

Oh, Lord, what kind of mess had she made? She must accept that they could be nothing more than friends or she'd drive Dirk away completely.

A soccer ball whizzed by, grazing Joni. "Sorry," called a little boy who didn't look particularly sorry.

Fred scooped up the ball and flung it onto the field. As Charlie caught it, his eyes met Joni's. His heavy lids and nearly invisible eyelashes gave his gaze a remote, inhuman quality. Then he tossed the ball into play, and a shouting mass of little boys battled for it. Had that been anger she saw on his face? she wondered. Or was she imagining it?

No one else appeared to have noticed anything amiss. Paranoia must be playing tricks on her.

DIRK PAGED THROUGH the data about Charlie Rogers. Age: 38. Marital status: Divorced. Military service in the navy. No children.

Two years ago, he'd moved from San Jose to Viento del Mar. He would have arrived just as Joni and Lowell were splitting up, so he could have read in the newspaper about her allegations that her husband was harassing her. Had he remembered the details and mimicked them later to discredit Lowell?

Through a service his business subscribed to, Dirk used Charlie's driver's license number to access his credit and police records. He found that the man hadn't told the whole truth about not having a criminal record.

There'd been one conviction for drunken driving and another for misdemeanor battery, no details provided. Then, three years ago, Charlie had been taken into custody for spousal abuse. As part of the sentencing, he'd had to complete an anger-management course. He'd also gotten a divorce.

The picture wasn't reassuring. Charlie Rogers had problems with alcohol and he'd beaten his wife.

Charlie had had an opportunity to throw paint at Dirk's car on Saturday. He would also have heard Kim's tirade against Joni. Plus, he presumably knew Del Mar Park well enough to have spied on Dirk and Joni on Sunday, then vanished when he was spotted.

On the other hand, the man hadn't exactly behaved like an ardent suitor, Dirk mused. He'd flirted with Joni previously and had brought flowers to the hospital. Still, aside from the way he'd glared at Dirk on Saturday, that didn't add up to much.

It was a long shot, but to be on the safe side, the police ought to check out his alibis for the times of the murders. And Joni should avoid being alone with him.

Dirk glanced at his watch; it was a minute past five. Nearly dark. She and Jeff would be leaving soccer practice soon. Although other people were likely to be around, he knew the killer was a master at manipulating people.

There was no way to contact her at the park short of going there himself. Dialing his cell phone as he walked, Dirk started for his car. He doubted a patrol officer would respond to his vague suspicions, so he put in a call directly to MacDougall. He got voice mail and left a terse message.

Outside, he couldn't spot his rental. It took several precious seconds to remember that he'd replaced it with a different model.

By the time he located it, the time on his watch clicked to 5:07.

THE SOCCER FAMILIES dispersed quickly into the cool night. Joni waited until Jeff retrieved his ball and started off with the Owenses before she headed in the other direction.

The rising ground blocked her view of the road. Only one streetlight marked her way and it cast more shadows than illumination. She hadn't realized the park could feel so isolated.

Off to her right, a figure moved into her range of vision. Her pulse pounding in her ears, Joni took another step and stumbled on a rough spot in the turf.

"You okay?" With two long strides, Charlie Rogers reached her. His hand closed over her arm with possessive tightness.

"Fine." Joni swallowed hard. She didn't want him to see how nervous she was.

"Where's Jeff?"

She wished she dared lie and say her son would be there any minute with Bobby's family in tow. But the field obviously stood deserted. "He went home with a friend."

"How's he taking all this?" The dim light gave the coach's square face a yellowish cast.

"All what?" Joni asked.

"A person can hardly help hearing what's on the news." He was so close she could smell peppermint gum on his breath.

With Charlie holding her arm, she couldn't move away unless she made a big production of it. Joni tried to shift backward unobtrusively, but he didn't release her. "He's taking it okay."

"And you?" he probed.

"Me?" She hated the way she kept responding with questions, but she couldn't concentrate on what he was asking.

A few minutes ago, they'd been surrounded. Now

there was only dimness and silence. All she could think about was getting over the rise to the street, where there'd be houses facing them and, presumably, people arriving home from work.

"Look, I know you're under a lot of stress." His jaw worked. "It's none of my business anyway. But you know, Joni, I don't like hearing gossip about you."

"Gossip?" Oh, Lord, if he would only let go!

"People are talking about you and your brother-in-law." His forehead creased. "You're a classy lady. I've admired you for some time. Why are you doing this?"

She decided to take the direct approach. "Would you walk me to my car?"

"There might be other people hanging around," he said. "I don't think you want them to hear this conversation."

"I don't care!" Joni tried to tug her arm free, but his grip tightened. The man had powerful hands; she remembered that he taught fitness classes. He probably worked out with weights, too.

"Why not? Because what they're saying is true?" He caught her other arm and swung her to face him. "Are you really that kind of woman, Joni?"

The movement pulled his sweater up enough for the dim light to glint off something thrust into his belt. Something hard and metallic.

A knife.

Chapter Fourteen

"Answer me!" He shook her. "I asked you a question!"

Where the fury came from, Joni didn't know. Welling up without warning, it galvanized her into action.

Her knee struck Charlie in the groin but not hard enough to hurt. It startled him, however, into releasing her arms, and she snatched at his ears, gripping them and digging in with her fingernails.

"What the—" Curses flew, but he couldn't jerk free without her nails ripping deeper into his ears.

Forcing his head down, Joni thrust upward with her knee and felt it connect with a crunch. With a curse, he shoved her back, and she stumbled to the ground. She scrambled for footing, but the darkness disoriented her and she staggered onto her knees. At any instant, she expected to feel the slash of a knife.

"I think you broke my damn nose!" Charlie gurgled from several feet away.

"Good!" Joni shouted.

On the street, a car door slammed. "Joni?" It was Dirk. "Joni, are you here?"

"Look out!" she yelled. "He's got a knife!"

"I—what?" Bent over, cradling his injured face,

Charlie appeared to be trying to shake his head. "It's just a Swiss Army knife."

"Put your hands up!" Dirk came over the rise, hands clenched in front of him as if holding a service revolver. It was too dark to see if he was really armed.

"Aw, jeez, man!" Charlie dabbed at the air with his hands, then sank onto the grass. "Call an ambulance."

Lurching to her feet, Joni hurried to Dirk's side. She heard the harsh rush of his breathing, and when she touched him to steady herself, she felt the tightness in his muscles.

She could also see that what he held in his hands wasn't a gun but a phone.

While Charlie continued to sit on the ground complaining, Dirk punched a button and put the phone to his ear. "Joni Peterson was just attacked at Del Mar Park. We need the police and we need an ambulance."

"Hey!" Charlie gasped. "She attacked *me!*"

"You grabbed me and shook me!" Joni snapped. "What did you think you were doing?" The pent-up tension of the past week intensified her anger.

"I just wanted to talk," he muttered.

"Like you used to talk to your ex-wife?" Dirk challenged.

"What?" Joni brushed away the tears.

"He's a wife abuser," he said.

"Man, I've changed."

"I suspect the police have heard that line before," Dirk returned sharply.

The man was sniveling now. "Look, I wanted to ask her out, that's all."

He didn't sound to Joni like the monster she'd been fearing all week. But then, she reminded herself, no doubt he could act harmless when it suited him.

A few minutes later, sirens shrilled toward them. A patrolman and two paramedics ran into view, followed a short time later by Detective MacDougall. He grimaced as he watched the patrolman slap handcuffs on Charlie. "Guess I was wrong about you two" was the only comment he offered.

DIRK COULDN'T BELIEVE he'd let Joni get that close to danger. He should've foreseen it or done more to prevent it.

Something had changed between them last night. Joni had plugged into a long-buried need, connecting him to her and, in an inexplicable way, to himself. The prospect of harm coming to her was intolerable.

Heck, how much of an explanation did he require? She was the mother of his child, essential to Jeff's happiness. If for no other reason, Dirk would have gladly laid down his life to preserve hers.

Fortunately, she didn't appear to have suffered more than a few scrapes. And it was a lucky break that their son had gone home with the Owenses before the incident.

In Charlie's trunk, police found a nearly empty can of water-soluble red paint, left over from decorating booths at a soccer fund-raising carnival the previous spring. Charlie admitted having thrown the contents onto Dirk's car out of jealousy but denied any involvement with the murders. For the moment, he was being held for assault. The police were getting more warrants to search his apartment and health-club locker.

After a round of questioning, Dirk and Joni went home. It was hard to believe, as they unlocked the door and went inside, that they didn't have to be afraid anymore.

Unless, of course, the police screwed up and released Charlie. "I'm staying tonight," Dirk said. "I'll sleep on the sofa bed."

Long lashes curtained Joni's eyes as she considered. He hoped she wasn't going to insist on staying alone because, in that case, he would sleep in his car outside.

She faced him across the den. "You don't have to stay on the sofa."

His body responded instantly, viscerally. After last night, he knew how warm her mouth would be and how quickly she would come to heat. But he didn't dare let down his guard again. In one day, he'd stumbled across Kim DeLong's body and nearly lost Joni to a man he should have suspected all along. What else had he overlooked?

"I'll be more alert if I stay by myself." He forced himself not to move toward her, not to touch.

"But Charlie's in custody."

"I'll feel better when the D.A.'s brought murder charges and a judge has denied bail," Dirk said. "Until then, he could get a lawyer to spring him."

She sighed. "I suppose you're right."

"By the way," he said, "Herb suggested you move back to the estate and offered to live there, too. If Mrs. Wright is a problem, I'll give her a pension or find her another job."

"This house does hold some terrible memories," Joni conceded. "But some wonderful ones, too." The look she gave him left no doubt what she was referring to.

"You'll think about Herb's offer?"

"Sure." Her expression softened. "Dirk, thank you. I'm so grateful you showed up tonight."

"You're the one who saved yourself."

"He made me mad. But...that was quite a trick with

the phone. That took guts." She came closer, her palm reaching to cup his cheek. Slowly, her thumb traced his temple and jawline.

Dirk held himself motionless, and then the flood burst. Fiercely, he caught her against him and invaded her mouth with his tongue. Claiming her, stamping her.

His body hardened as she responded with silky sweetness. Beneath her clothes, he could feel her moving to a seductive beat. Inviting him to a private dance.

Then what? Dirk asked himself harshly. He couldn't promise her a future. Last night, he'd operated on pure instinct. Tonight, he had no such excuse. He had never felt as close to anyone as he did to Joni. All the more reason to avoid giving cause for bitterness. More than anything in the world, he needed to keep her as his friend.

When the kiss ended, he stepped regretfully away. "I don't want to make promises I can't keep. Let's leave it at that, Joni."

In her expressive face, he saw disappointment, but no anger. "What made you so gun-shy? Was it...that woman you mentioned?"

"Partly," Dirk said. "Her death made me face what kind of person I am and what kind of life I need. Sooner or later, I'd let you down, too. I don't want that to happen."

She released a long breath. "Once you're sure the police will hold Charlie, you'll be going away, won't you?"

Once, he'd loved the prospect of flying off to new places. Now he thought with displeasure of the dry air inside a jet, stiff plastic seat cushions and tough, flash-frozen food. Foreign airline terminals weren't romantic.

They reeked of cigarette smoke, and the flight announcements echoed incomprehensibly.

Excitement. Adventure. Emptiness.

Yet beyond the tedium of air travel lay a wild unknown that stirred Dirk's adrenaline and made him most truly himself. He needed the challenge. He needed the freedom.

"Yes," he said. "I'll only be a phone call away if you need me. I'm sorry I can't promise more."

Her lips curved into a weary smile. "My father never told us he was leaving. At least with you, I'll have a phone number. I guess that qualifies as an improvement."

When she said good-night and walked away, Dirk stood rooted to the spot. He wished she had slapped him. It would have hurt less.

BY THE TIME JONI GOT dressed on Thursday morning, she discovered Dirk was ready to go out. He had a long day ahead, he said. Two potential buyers wanted to see the Peterson estate, and he'd decided to keep the printing company in the family for Jeff's sake.

That meant whipping it into shape for someone else to step in, then finding that someone. He wanted to interview top employees as well as contact an executive search service.

At the door, he gave Joni one wistful glance and then he was gone. Not even a kiss.

Rationally, she knew he had a point. Lovers built up layers of emotion that could explode; friendship was steadier and more enduring. She didn't care. She wanted to enjoy every scrap of time together while they could. But there was no use beating her head against a brick wall.

After collecting the newspaper, Joni went inside to eat and read. The front page, as expected, was full of news about Kim DeLong's death and the arrest of Charlie Rogers. Apparently, he'd suffered a bloody nose but not a broken one, she learned.

Silence lengthened through the house as she finished her cereal and coffee. Suddenly, she ached to see her son.

She called Kathryn. "Did you hear about Charlie?" she asked right after saying hello.

"Yes!" Her friend sounded breathless. "I can't believe it. I mean, he was so nice to the kids. But I'm glad it's over."

"You two have been wonderful through this whole thing," Joni said. "Why don't I pick up the boys at day care, fix dinner and take them trick-or-treating? They can sleep over, too. You and Fred deserve a night to yourselves."

"We could use some time together," Kathryn agreed. "But aren't you and Dirk going to celebrate your birthday?"

Her birthday. Thirty years old. "I've been trying not to think about it," Joni admitted. Dirk hadn't said a word. She couldn't remember whether he even knew it was her birthday. "I'd like to celebrate with the kids, if that's okay with you. I'll take them both to school in the morning, too."

"That would be great." From the relief in Kathryn's voice, Joni realized she must have been feeling stressed.

At the back door came a light, rapid tapping. "That sounds like my neighbor," Joni said. "I'll see you later."

"Thanks again!" Her friend rang off.

Sure enough, it was Celia, her arms filled with small packages. "Happy birthday, Joni!"

"I can't believe you remembered!" Hoping that she wasn't going to be late for work but appreciative of her neighbor's kindness, Joni invited her inside. "What a delightful surprise!"

The older woman smiled, clearly enjoying herself as she presented each parcel in turn. "These are Chinese bean-curd pastries, not too sweet. I hope you like the flavor."

"I'm sure I will."

The next package, topped with clear cellophane, contained four round green fruits. "Asian pears," Celia explained. "You peel them and slice them. They taste like pears but they are crisp." Next, a box of pineapple-flavored cakes joined the gifts on the table.

Joni thanked her profusely, then said, "I wish I had more time to visit, but my boss must be getting impatient. Could you come over Saturday afternoon for coffee?"

"I look forward to it." Celia patted her on the arm. "I am so glad they arrested that man. Now you are safe." She glanced toward the den. "Is your brother-in-law still here?"

"He went to work." It didn't seem enough of an explanation, so Joni added, "He'll be leaving town soon. His business is overseas."

Her neighbor smiled. "Like my husband. But you are too smart to marry someone who is always gone. Well, I see you Saturday!"

After ushering her outside, Joni collected her purse. She still couldn't bring herself to take her own lunch, though.

How *had* Charlie managed to slip inside the hospital

on Tuesday and put the fringe in her bag? she wondered. Perhaps he'd been making plumbing repairs.

On the way out, she remembered to set her new alarm system. Yesterday afternoon, she'd been in such a hurry to pick up Jeff for the soccer game that she'd forgotten. It might take a while to get used to this thing, which was ironic considering that her reason for installing it no longer existed.

Fog lay heavy on the ground, and Joni navigated her car with care. On San Bernardo Road, a scarecrow dangling from a tree startled her even though she'd seen it before. In light of the two recent murders, she wished whoever had chosen this ghoulish decoration would display better judgment.

At the hospital, a couple of people stopped her to ask if she'd been hurt yesterday and to express relief about the arrest. It helped the reality sink in that she no longer had to fear being stalked.

Joni's mood lightened further as she observed the costumes that many of the staff wore for the holiday. Although hospital policy discouraged anything that might interfere with patient care, workers indulged in face paints, shocking hair colors and offbeat sweatshirts.

Black and orange crepe paper festooned the public relations office, Joni noted as she arrived. When Basil padded from his office, she saw that he was chewing an unlit pipe and wearing a Sherlock Holmes cap and a tweed jacket with elbow patches.

"What do you think?" he asked.

"It suits you." She regarded his tall, gaunt frame. He *did* remind her somewhat of the legendary detective.

He cleared his throat, a sign that he was about to raise a more or less personal issue. "How are you holding up? The radio said you were assaulted."

"My knees are scraped, but you should see the other guy." Joni couldn't help chuckling. "Honest, I gave worse than I got."

"That's over, then." Her boss made a satisfied clucking noise. "In that case—"

"—you can expect me to get the newsletter out on time after all," she finished for him.

"Er, yes," he said.

Joni went to work at her computer. She lost track of time until the hospital florist appeared about ten o'clock with a large flower arrangement in black and orange. It was spectacular but, she reflected, a touch creepy.

"Is there a card?" she asked, giving him a tip.

"Right in there." He pointed to a small orange envelope. "Happy Halloween."

"Thanks."

Inside the envelope she found a white card. It read, "Glad they got the killer, but I hope you'll still consider living on the estate or buying a new house together so I can watch over you and Jeff. Happy birthday!" It was signed, "Herb."

Joni studied the note with mixed feelings. If money were no object, she'd be happy to consider moving to a different house, but the Peterson mansion retained too many memories of Lowell. She doubted she could ever feel comfortable there.

It was kind of Herb to offer to leave his condo development, where he enjoyed the games and classes sponsored by a senior citizens' club. And it *would* be nice for Jeff to have a father figure on the premises. She couldn't help reflecting that, in fact, he had a father, but one who wouldn't be around for long. The thought made her chest ache.

In some other lifetime, she and Dirk might have been

destined to be together. But not in this one. The chasm between them was too great.

He bore the scars of a youth filled with his father's tyranny and rejection. Even the death of a woman he loved hadn't been enough to cure his restlessness.

Had he felt about this woman the way he felt about her? She supposed it was impossible to compare the two relationships at such different points in his life.

What she needed wasn't a man to lean on at every turn but an unshakable bond with someone she loved. Someone who would be there for her and Jeff when it counted, in the ways that mattered most.

Dirk seemed to think that was what he was offering. But he was holding back the essential part of himself. His love. His intimacy. His commitment.

She wondered how long it would take before she could regard him as someone whose absences didn't matter, and whose presence brought only mild pleasure. Would that ever be possible?

After setting the flowers on a side table, Joni returned to work. At lunchtime, she made a quick trip to the cafeteria and brought back a sandwich so she could continue editing.

In her distracted state, she had to rewrite more than usual and juggle the layout several times. By late afternoon, several hours of work remained, but at least she would be able to finish by midday Friday. Then she could drop the camera-ready art at Peterson Printing and pick it up on Monday. She would make her deadline. Barely.

By four o'clock, the part-time secretary had left for the day, so when the phone rang, Joni answered it herself. "Public relations."

"Mrs. Peterson? Detective MacDougall." Did she just imagine that his voice held an ominous note?

Her hands went cold. "Is something wrong?"

"We've released Charlie Rogers."

She couldn't believe it. "He made bail?"

"He's been released on his own recognizance," the detective said. "I'm afraid the only charges we can bring are simple assault and malicious mischief."

The receiver nearly slipped from her grasp. "What do you mean?"

"We can't link him to either of the murders." A trace of huskiness hinted at the detective's frustration. "Last Wednesday, at the time your husband was killed, Mr. Rogers was conducting an aerobics class. We have a dozen witnesses."

Her mind searched frantically. "What about Saturday?"

"He says he was home alone. That's not much of an alibi, but there's nothing to tie him to Mrs. DeLong," the policeman said. "No witnesses, no evidence."

"His knife?"

"We ran tests. It's clean."

She yearned to feel safe a little while longer. "Can't you hold him for a day or so?"

"He got out half an hour ago." MacDougall sighed. "I was just informed and I thought you'd want to know."

"Yes. Thank you." Numbly, Joni hung up. Into her mind flashed the scene from last night: the isolated soccer field, the eerie shadows from a distant streetlight.

Charlie had threatened her and grabbed her. How could they let him go?

But a man couldn't be in two places at once. If a

dozen students confirmed that he'd been teaching aerobics, she didn't see how he could have murdered Lowell.

It was time to stop clutching at straws. Unwillingly, Joni forced herself to face the facts.

Charlie Rogers couldn't be the killer. That meant her stalker hadn't been arrested.

He was still out there.

Chapter Fifteen

The first of the two potential buyers, a tall, balding man with a handlebar mustache, arrived on schedule at the Peterson estate and proceeded to criticize everything from its winding driveway to the lack of a swimming pool. After a teeth-gritting hour and a half, both Dirk and the real-estate agent were relieved to see him go.

He'd encroached into the second prospect's time, but that didn't matter because she arrived late. Very late, towing her mother, her sister, her brother-in-law and two small children.

They loved the property, if only Dirk would agree to sell it for half price. And, in lieu of a down payment, to trade for a property they'd inherited in the Mojave Desert.

Leaving the agent to shoo them away, he drove to the printing plant in an edgy mood. Dirk wasn't sure what had set him off; the buyers were a pain, but he'd encountered their types before in his various business ventures: the nitpicker and the wheeler-dealer.

He cheered himself by reflecting back to his morning's review of the company books. Profits had risen steadily, costs had been kept at a reasonable level, and Lowell's publishing prospectus was exciting.

Best of all, Joni's stalker had been captured and put behind bars. She and Jeff were safe.

At least with you, I'll have a phone number. I guess that qualifies as an improvement.

The memory of her words seared Dirk. Joni hadn't intended to taunt him by comparing him to her runaway father, he felt sure. She'd merely been stating a fact, and that made it all the worse.

How could he reconcile his feelings for her, and for Jeff, with what he knew of his own nature? It would be worse to make a commitment and then break it than to make none at all. But it was also possible, Dirk knew, that he was simply afraid to risk everything on one roll of the dice.

Turning into the parking lot, he headed for his reserved space and nearly drove into the yellow police tape that roped it off. As he hit the brakes, his heart started to race with unexpected anxiety.

Taking a deep breath, he parked alongside the building. He hadn't given himself a chance to recover from finding Kim's body yesterday. No matter how tough a man imagined himself to be, a shock like that was bound to affect him.

What kind of a monster was Charlie Rogers anyway? Had he truly believed he would impress Joni by killing her one-time rival?

Mulling over that question, he exited the car and strode inside. When he entered the administrative wing, a stocky man in a tailored suit rose to greet him.

"Maynard!" Dirk shook hands enthusiastically. "What brings you here?"

Maynard Greenburg, a voluble man in his forties, headed a Los Angeles advertising and marketing firm that specialized in adapting promotions to local tastes anywhere in the world. He'd flown to out-of-the-way sites several times to meet Dirk and formulate strategies for boosting new businesses.

"Actually, I had an appointment with your brother," the man said. "He contacted me about writing a book for him. Your secretary just told me about his death. I'm very sorry."

"I regret that you had to get the news this way," Dirk said. "If I'd known about your appointment, I'd have called."

"It wasn't on my calendar," the secretary said apologetically. "Mr. Peterson must have forgotten to tell me."

"Now that you mention it, I remember recommending you to him," Dirk told Maynard. "I figured you'd be worth a couple of book ideas at least. Come on in. I apologize for keeping you waiting."

"No problem. I'm spending a few days in Santa Barbara with my daughter, so I didn't have to drive all that far."

"You have messages, Mr. Peterson!" the secretary called as they went into Dirk's private office.

"Thanks. I'll look at them later." He couldn't wait to go over ideas with Maynard. A writer this inventive and cutting edge would be perfect to help launch the publishing venture.

The discussion flowed. Dirk took copious notes, only wishing he would be on hand to see the project carried to fulfillment. On the other hand, it might take quite a while to find an executive to run the company and serve as publisher, and he would have to fill in until then. Dirk was surprised how much that prospect pleased him.

By the time Maynard departed, he discovered to his

surprise that the daylight had gone. So had his secretary, since it was nearly six o'clock.

For the past few days, Dirk had always been aware on some level that he needed to keep tabs on Joni's safety. Today, he'd cut himself some slack because that was no longer necessary.

Messages. Right.

He punched a command into his computer and the secretary's notes appeared. First, a major order was expected, and the foreman wanted his approval to reserve sufficient paper stock at the mill. Second, he needed to authorize the annual Christmas merit bonuses.

The third one was from Joni. "They've released Charlie Rogers. He has an alibi for last Wednesday."

Dirk pictured the short-haired man sitting on the grass last night, clutching his injured face and whining. He'd all but attacked Joni and he had a violent history.

Surely the police wouldn't have let him go unless the alibi was airtight. Their killer, however, might be clever enough to fake an alibi.

He put in a call to MacDougall and got his voice mail. The man had left for the day.

Where was Joni? Dirk tried her house, but the answering machine picked up. A call to the hospital public relations office brought the same result. She must be in transit. There was no reason to believe she faced any immediate danger, and yet…

He glanced out the window and remembered that it was Halloween. Rationally or not, Joni had believed matters would come to a head tonight.

It was also her thirtieth birthday. A turning point, a milestone in her life.

Any man who wanted to possess her badly enough to kill would surely intend to be part of this night. While

Charlie's arrest made everyone complacent, the real killer could have been watching his chance and moving into position.

Joni was in danger; Dirk had no doubt of that. He grabbed his coat and headed for the door.

CARRYING THE OVERSIZE floral arrangement, Joni hurried down the hospital corridor. In her eagerness to finish screening photographs for the newsletter, she'd lost track of time, and the day-care center closed at six.

She hustled past the auditorium, where the Red Cross had chosen this rather ghoulish night to hold a blood donor clinic. It amused her, when she glanced inside, to see a man in a Dracula costume filling out his paperwork to give blood.

"Joni!"

She glanced up, startled. From the auditorium emerged a white-coated volunteer, none other than Herb.

"Oh, hi!" She smiled at Dirk's grandfather. "Thanks for the flowers!"

"Need some help with those?"

Joni was about to decline when she realized she really did need help. "Sure. Thanks."

Herb moved ahead of her to the heavy glass door and propped it open. "I just heard on the radio about them letting that coach go. I think it's terrible."

"Apparently he's innocent," she said. "Of murder anyway." A breeze misted her face, reminding her that showers were expected. The air felt ominously heavy, the way it had last Wednesday. The night Lowell was killed.

The older man relieved her of the flowers and walked beside her between rows of parked cars. "Do you have anything special planned tonight? I thought I might drop by later.''

"That would be lovely.'' She stopped beside her sedan. ''I'm taking Jeff and Bobby trick-or-treating, but we should be finished by eight. Probably earlier if this rain gets worse.''

"You mean that grandson of mine isn't planning a special celebration for your birthday?'' he asked.

Joni fished the key from her purse. Herb was perceptive enough to have noticed that she and Dirk were far from indifferent to each other, but she hoped he didn't guess how involved they'd become.

"Not that I know of.'' After setting the flowers in the passenger seat, she slid behind the wheel. Herb closed the door and leaned on it, watching her.

"Joni, I want to talk to you about the future,'' he said. ''Your plans, I mean.''

If she were more than ten minutes late to fetch the children, the center would bill her extra. A lot extra.

"I'm sorry but I've got to pick up the boys. Can we talk later? Please?'' She turned the key in the ignition.

Nothing happened. Not even a click.

Joni's stomach sank. She tried again. Still nothing.

Urgently, she considered her options. A jump-start? A cab?

"I'll give you a ride,'' Herb said.

"Aren't they depending on you at the blood drive?'' she asked.

"We can pick up the boys and I'll drop you off at home,'' he said. ''I'll be back before anyone notices I'm gone.''

She didn't feel right, taking him away from his volunteer duties. During the hospital's blood drives, the early evening hours were always the busiest.

Down the aisle cruised a white minivan with black and silver racing stripes. With a rush of relief, Joni recognized it, and the driver. "That's Bobby's dad!"

"I've met him," Herb said stiffly. "What's he doing here?"

"Keeping his mother company, I presume. She has dialysis a couple of times a week." At Joni's wave, the van halted directly in front of her.

The window hummed down. "What's up?" Fred called across the passenger seat.

She told him.

"No problem. I'll jump-start your car and follow you to the garage. We don't want you getting stranded along the way." He lifted his cell phone to his ear. "I'll ask Kathryn to run by the day-care center and meet us at your house. We can pick up fast food for everybody."

Joni hated to impose, especially when she'd planned to give the Owenses a night off, but it was a sensible way to deal with the situation. "That should work out fine. Herb, thanks, but I know they need you inside."

The older man yielded. "As long as someone's looking after you." He strolled toward the building, not seeming to mind the rain pattering around him.

It had turned into a downpour by the time Fred got her car started. The motor sputtered alarmingly, and Joni was grateful that her garage was only a block away.

They arrived just as the mechanic was leaving. He let her put the car inside and promised to work on it first thing in the morning.

Fred's wipers arced across the windshield in a steady beat, welcoming Joni to the van. He smiled as he watched her put the flower arrangement in back.

"That's right, it's your thirtieth birthday, isn't it?" he

said. "Such a special occasion. You know, I'm glad I have a chance to celebrate it with you."

Reaching across the seat, he patted her hand.

DIRK WAS CROSSING the outer office when the phone rang. On the verge of ignoring it, he realized that it might be Joni.

"Peterson Printing, Dirk speaking," he said into the mouthpiece.

"Thank goodness I reached you!" The woman's voice was sharp with tension. "This is Kathryn Owens, Bobby's mother. Do you know where Joni is?"

Fear coalesced inside him. "She's not answering the phone at home or at work. Why? What's happened?"

"She promised to pick up the boys, but the day-care director just called," Kathryn said. "She's late, which isn't like her."

He checked his watch. Ten past six. Even if he'd just missed Joni at the hospital, she should have reached the center by now.

"I'll run over to the hospital and retrace her route," he said. "You'll get the kids?"

"Of course," Kathryn said. "I'll take them to the Halloween party at the church." She gave him the phone number there. "And, Dirk…"

"Yes?"

"I didn't want to speak out of turn, and maybe this isn't relevant, but…"

What key piece of information had this woman been sitting on? Dirk's instincts screamed at him to reach across the phone line and shake her, but instead he said with tight control, "Tell me everything. Quickly."

"Fred and I have been having some problems." Strain made her tone high and thin. "He's Bobby's stepfather.

My first husband died in a car crash. I didn't know much about Fred before we got married five years ago. He lived with his mother, and she's really nice. I met her at the supermarket where I work.''

They didn't have time for Kathryn's life story. "Is there something you've learned about him? Something that makes you suspicious?"

"Nothing definite," she said. "I thought it was odd that his driver's license gives his name as Frederick Owens but on some of his papers it's Allen Frederick Owens. Also, I came across two social security cards with different numbers."

"Can you read them out to me?" Using a middle name as a first name might not be unusual, but honest people didn't carry two social security cards.

"Just a minute." Time dragged until she picked up the phone again. "Here they are." She gave him the numbers.

"Anything else?" Dirk asked.

Kathryn made a noise that was almost a sob. "He plays basketball a lot of nights, or that's what he says he's doing, but I don't know whom he plays with or where, and he gets angry when I ask. That's not all. I feel so stupid. I—I didn't want to make the connection, I didn't mention anything to Joni and now—"

"What else?" The words rapped out harshly. "What else, Kathryn?"

"Two of my kitchen knives are missing," she said. "The first one, I thought I'd just misplaced it, but I haven't been able to find the second one since I fixed dinner on Saturday."

Kim DeLong had been stabbed to death that same night. So far, the murder weapon hadn't turned up.

"Go get the boys." Dirk needed to make sure Jeff

was taken care of. "I'll handle the rest. Is he driving your van?"

"Yes. Please hurry." She sounded scared.

He didn't even know for sure that Fred was anywhere near Joni, Dirk reminded himself as he raced to his car. Nevertheless, he dialed the police as he took off for the hospital.

RAIN MUST HAVE BEEN falling heavily in the mountains inland, because Viento del Mar Creek was spilling over its banks. It had narrowed San Bernardo Road to one lane in each direction.

"What a mess," Fred said as they inched forward in a line of steaming cars.

"Maybe we should forget about stopping for food," Joni said. "I hate to make Kathryn wait. She doesn't even have a key to my house."

"She can use the one you hide," Fred said.

"It's not there anymore." Joni peered out into a blur of passing lights. "Anyway, I changed the locks."

"Smart move." He seemed remarkably jovial, considering that most men would be pounding their horns by this time. "We can't have you going hungry on such an important occasion."

"Oh, I can always find something in the fridge," she said. "But I suppose you're right. We don't want the boys to fill up on candy."

After the two eastbound lanes funneled into one, the traffic picked up. Through the rain, the oncoming headlights and neon signs formed a blurry glare.

As they crossed the bridge, it struck Joni that in the three years since Bobby and Jeff met at school, she'd never been alone with Fred before. Or if she had, the occasion hadn't stuck in her memory.

She glanced at him and found that, even now, it was hard to think of Fred apart from the roles of Kathryn's husband and Bobby's father. Everything about him, from his light brown hair and pleasantly rounded face to the spreading waistline, seemed designed to blend into a crowd.

All she knew about his background was that he'd once aspired to play professional baseball and that he remained strongly attached to his mother. Fred was, she guessed, in his early forties, and he and Kathryn must have been married at least nine years in order to have an eight-year-old son.

The van eased into the drive-through line of a fried-chicken restaurant. Around the building's eaves, Halloween decorations sagged in the rain.

"How's your mother?" Joni asked. When Fred continued staring at the taillights ahead of them, she added, "I know dialysis patients sometimes have a hard time accepting their dependence on a machine."

"Oh, she doesn't mind the machine as much as the dietary restrictions." Turning toward her, he studied Joni. "Say, why don't we skip this and I'll take you to the Chalet for a steak? That would be more festive."

"The Chalet?" The town's most expensive restaurant sat on a hill several miles out of town. "What about Kathryn and the kids?"

He laughed. "I almost forgot them! Must be something about you, Joni. You could make a man lose his head."

Gooseflesh prickled her arms. Obviously, Fred was joking, but didn't he realize how creepy it sounded?

They reached the order window, and she had to concentrate on which side dishes to select and how many drinks they needed. Then she and Fred fished out their wallets; she wanted to pay, but he wouldn't let her.

"It's my treat," he said. "Then let's stop at a bakery and I'll buy you a birthday cake. What do you say?"

"Thanks, but I'd rather get home." Joni was relieved when he didn't press the point.

The server handed him a cardboard bucket, several paper sacks and a cardboard tray of drinks. The smell of fried chicken filled the van.

Fred stuffed the food containers around her and placed the drink holder in her lap. She felt trapped, but she wasn't sure why.

As they turned onto the main road, Joni became increasingly nervous. The hazardous driving conditions must be affecting her appetite because she was no longer even hungry.

Something dark swung toward the windshield. With a thump, a hideous grinning face hit the glass. Joni shrieked. The drink tray slid toward the floor. She grabbed it, barely in time.

A scarecrow. The dangling figure must have torn loose from its ties and hit the car.

"There ought to be a law against that kind of thing," she grumbled. "We could've had an accident."

"I found it kind of exciting." Fred wore an expression that bordered on gloating. "Don't you enjoy the sense of danger?"

"Not particularly." Why was he talking this way? Usually he understood her feelings and offered helpful insights. Tonight, Fred seemed like a different person.

Joni's muscles tensed so hard her ribs ached. Alarm bells jangled in every nerve ending.

Painfully, she forced herself to examine the odd way Fred was behaving. Patting her hand, tucking the food around her, offering to take her to the Chalet. Most of all, wearing an air of triumph. He clearly enjoyed having her to himself and being in control of the situation.

The clues were all there; she just hadn't put them together, she realized with a jolt. Or was she getting carried away as she'd done with Charlie?

Fred had overheard Kim's tirade against her after the soccer game on Saturday. He also knew she kept a key hidden behind the house. He could have used it to get inside on Sunday.

Two days ago, Edith Owens had finished her dialysis session at lunchtime. If Fred had dropped by to visit during her session, he would have been in the hospital at the right time to tamper with Joni's lunch.

Fred? Could Fred be the killer?

She tried to get a grip on her fears. It wasn't a fool-proof case, not by a long shot. Most likely, he had alibis for the times of the murders.

The van turned into Canyon Acres. Her panic abated.

They were only a few blocks from home. Kathryn and the boys would be waiting.

Chapter Sixteen

The dispatcher said Detective MacDougall was still in the field but offered to transfer Dirk to the watch commander. He thanked her and kept the phone pressed to his ear as he waited.

Although the printing plant lay only half a mile from the hospital, he'd been crawling through traffic for ten minutes. The way the rain was coming down, the situation could only get worse. He had to reach someone who could do something.

"Sergeant Cruz," a woman's voice announced in his ear.

"This is Dirk Peterson," he said. "Joni Peterson is missing and I've just learned that a family friend may be hiding a criminal history."

Since he hadn't stopped to check on Fred in the computer, Dirk was making a broad assumption. He didn't care. He would rather risk being wrong than lose Joni from an excess of caution.

"What is this individual's name?" the sergeant asked. She didn't ask who Joni was or what was going on; she must be well aware of the case.

"Frederick Owens. He also uses the name Allen Frederick Owens," Dirk said. "He has a couple of different social security numbers, and his wife is missing two knives from her kitchen.''

''Are you saying he's abducted Mrs. Peterson?''

''I don't know,'' he admitted. ''But she failed to pick up her son after work. Owens knew her schedule, and his wife can't locate him.''

''Do you have a description of his and Mrs. Peterson's vehicles?''

He provided them, along with the social security numbers. Computer keys clicked as she entered the information. ''Joni should've left her job at the hospital an hour ago,'' he added. ''I'm trying to get there, but the traffic's terrible.''

''We're working a lot of accidents and the creek's flooding,'' the sergeant said. ''I'll call Detective MacDougall in the field and put out an APB on both subject vehicles. Is there a number where I can reach you?''

Dirk gave it to her.

''Let us know if you find Mrs. Peterson,'' she said. ''I hope this is a false alarm.''

''You and me both,'' he said.

The conversation failed to reassure him. The storm had already spread the police too thin, and he doubted they would treat Joni's disappearance as an emergency. Lots of people might be temporarily missing tonight, thanks to the weather.

Minutes dragged by until, at last, he turned into the hospital. Whipping into a space marked for emergencies, Dirk yanked out the key and ran inside.

In the lobby, he stopped a candy striper. ''I need to find Joni Peterson. It's urgent. She works in the—''

''I know where she works,'' said the teenager, a pretty

African-American girl with a serious expression. "I'll take you there." She moved quickly ahead of him.

The public relations office was locked and dark. Dirk smacked his hand against the wall in frustration.

The candy striper considered for a moment. "There's a blood donor drive tonight. Maybe she stopped to donate."

Unlikely, but he might as well check. "Where is it?"

The teenager sprinted beside him along another corridor. Near the end, signs pointed donors toward an auditorium. After wishing him luck, the girl returned to her duties.

Dirk's gaze swept the large room. People waited on folding chairs; nurses in white tended the donors; volunteers took medical histories at a couple of tables. No sign of Joni.

At the aftercare table, Herb was pouring juice. Catching sight of Dirk, he set down the pitcher and whisked toward him. "You looking for Joni?" Herb asked. "She left half an hour ago."

Relief rushed through Dirk. "She's all right, then?"

"Sure, she's all right." His grandfather regarded him quizzically. "Something wrong?"

"Her friend Kathryn called. Joni didn't show up at the day-care center."

"Kathryn?" Herb's eyebrows rose in dismay. "Kathryn Owens?"

Dirk's anxiety returned, full force. "You sound surprised."

"Her husband said he was going to call and have her get the kids," the older man said.

"You talked to Fred?"

"Joni's car wouldn't start," Herb said. "Fred happened by and offered her a ride."

Fear tightened Dirk's throat. Fred hadn't called Kathryn. There could only be one reason why he would have lied.

"It's him," he said. "He's the killer."

THE HOUSE SAT ON THE HILL, barely discernible against the dark backdrop of trees. No lights shone at this end of the street, not even at Celia's place. To Joni, her home looked desolate and forlorn.

In the heavy rain, there was no sign of trick-or-treaters. None of the usual evening joggers and dog walkers would brave this kind of deluge, either. Right now, Joni wished the press *were* harassing her; at least there might be someone hanging around.

As the van turned into her driveway, she tried to spot Kathryn's station wagon. When they crested the rise, her last hope died. The turnaround was empty.

"They're not here yet," she said.

"No?" Fred didn't sound surprised. "Maybe they decided to go to the church party instead."

He knew as well as she did that Kathryn wouldn't change plans without notifying them. Joni could hardly breathe.

Frantically, she tried to remember what Fred had said on his end of the phone conversation. But he'd placed the call from inside his van; she hadn't heard any of it.

He might not have called Kathryn at all.

Come to think of it, why had he been driving through the hospital parking lot at six o'clock? On Tuesday, Edith Owens had undergone dialysis in the morning. Why, two days later, would her son be visiting her in the evening?

Maybe he'd known Joni would be stranded and would

need a ride. Maybe he'd disabled her car and driven around until she showed up.

Disbelief clouded her mind. She'd known this man for three years, trusted him with her son, become friends with his wife.

Fred switched off the engine. Rain sheeted against the roof and windows, isolating them.

When he turned toward Joni, she saw a face different from the one she knew. Subtle changes—a slackness of skin tone, a fixedness of the eyes, a looseness about the mouth—transformed Fred Owens into a stranger.

She swallowed hard. Instinctively, she tried not to let him see that she'd noticed anything. Maybe if she pretended everything was normal, he wouldn't take action.

"We need to call Kathryn," she said. "To make sure she's picked up the kids."

"Forget Kathryn," he said.

"Then we should go to the day-care center ourselves."

"This is our special time." His voice took on a wheedling quality, with a threat lingering below the surface. "Don't ruin it, Joni. Don't make me punish you again."

"Is that what you were doing?" It corresponded to what Dirk had surmised, yet she could still hardly comprehend it. "Framing me for murder? Breaking into my house, threatening me at work?"

"I knew they'd never charge you with murder," he said. "You needed to be taught a lesson. You're too independent, Joni. You need to let me take charge now."

"I don't understand." But she did, all too well. He wanted to control and dominate her. Dirk had been right.

"It's your birthday," Fred went on in that same hypnotic tone. "Turning thirty, that's important. It's when you put your mistakes behind you and start over."

"It is?" She wished she had a weapon. Or at least some way to bolt out of the van without having to extricate herself from all this food.

He leaned against his armrest, perfectly at ease. "When I turned thirty, Mom and I were living in Phoenix. The women I met there, well, they were low class. I decided to start over in a clean place. That's the special thing about this birthday, Joni. It's a chance to make a fresh start. With me."

She didn't want a fresh start; she wanted to get away from him. How could he possibly fantasize a future together after he'd murdered two people?

She didn't want to antagonize him. The best thing would be to keep him talking, and maybe Celia would come home. Or Dirk.

An image formed in her mind, of Dirk's dark head bending over her, his blue eyes bright with concern. It steadied her.

"After we left Phoenix," Fred went on, "we tried L.A., but I didn't like it. Nothing but trash. I needed a small town where you can really get to know people. So we drove up the coast. Mom fell in love with this place and so did I."

His fingers stroked her wrist. With all her strength, Joni resisted the urge to snatch her hand away.

"When I met Kathryn, I thought at first I'd found the right woman," he said. "She seemed like such a nice widow lady with a little boy."

"Bobby isn't your son?" Joni wasn't sure why that made a difference. But neither Fred nor Kathryn had mentioned the fact in the three years she'd known them, which meant he must have wanted it kept secret.

He liked to play roles, she realized. He liked to hide

who he really was. It must give him a sense of superiority; it certainly had enabled him to fool people.

"At first, I had fun playing with the little boy, but now that he's getting older, he's annoying. Whiny, like his mother," Fred said. "Besides, Jeff's a better soccer player. He's more athletic. Like me."

In your dreams!

"When I met you, I knew I'd found the right girl." Fred leaned over, and his breath whispered across her neck. Joni gritted her teeth to keep from flinching. "More beautiful, more intelligent. You were married then, but I could see you weren't happy. It was just a question of time."

For three years he'd been stalking her, at least in his mind. Pretending to be her friend. Spending time with her son, giving her advice.

Lowell had come to her house, his last night on earth, to try to catch her stalker. Had he been able to see, in the moments before he died, that it was Fred? How terrible for him, not even to be able to warn her. She had to stop tormenting herself. She had to figure out what to do.

"Lowell was a selfish, low-class jerk," Fred said. "Aren't you glad I protected you from him after the way he treated you? And Kim DeLong. She deserved what she got."

He had killed Kim out of some misplaced sense of loyalty to Joni? She bit her lip in dismay. But she had to concentrate on keeping the man talking while she formulated a plan.

"Why didn't you leave your wife?" she asked. "Why didn't you simply tell me how you felt?"

He blinked as if the thought had never occurred to

him. "What difference does it make? We're here now, aren't we? Just the two of us."

He seemed awfully certain that Dirk wouldn't show up. What if Fred had done something to him?

A vise clamped across Joni's chest. She had to find out even if it angered the man. "But you know my brother-in-law has been staying here."

"He left," Fred said. "I saw him go back to his old home. That was a wise decision, Joni. I'm glad you threw him out."

So Fred had been spying on Dirk today. He must have seen him going to show the estate to buyers, she thought, and tried to hide her relief.

Dirk was safe. But he might be working late or stuck in traffic. For all she knew, he might still believe Charlie was in custody.

Fred's fingers crept up her cheek and brushed back some loose strands of hair. Fear and disgust made Joni start to shake.

"Are you cold, darling?" he whispered. "We should go inside."

She remembered the security system. The alarm was wired to the police station as well as rigged for earsplitting loudness. If she opened the door and punched in the wrong code, it would sound in—how long? A minute? Would people realize it wasn't a false alarm? How long would it take the police to get here?

As soon as it went off, Fred would know that she'd tricked him. Before it sounded, she would have to find some excuse to walk toward the utility room, then dash out the back door. But after that?

She couldn't think that far ahead. It was useless to worry; she just had to act.

"I guess I did get chilled," she said. "You're right. We should go in."

Fred grinned as if she'd given him the most wonderful present of his life. Or was about to.

DIRK WAS INCHING HIS CAR past the high school when his cell phone rang. He snatched it from his pocket. "Peterson here."

"MacDougall." Red taillights flashed ahead, and Dirk tapped the brakes. "The watch commander filled me in. You think she's with Owens?"

"I know she is." He relayed what he'd learned from Herb.

"Sergeant Cruz ran a check," the detective said. "Allen Frederick Owens has a dishonorable discharge from the marines and a couple of convictions in Arizona for assault and battery. He's also wanted for murder."

"A woman?"

"Ex-girlfriend. Or at least she was trying to leave." MacDougall uttered a curse. "He's had us chasing our tails all over town. I've been talking to some of Mrs. DeLong's friends and my car's stuck in the mud out near the country club. Any idea where he might take her?"

Dirk had instinctively driven toward Canyon Acres. "He seems to want to stake his claim, not kill her. If I'm right, he'll head for her house. Does your department have a helicopter?"

"Are you kidding?" MacDougall said. "Even if we did, it couldn't fly in this weather. I'll radio for a patrol car ASAP."

Unless there was one already in the vicinity, Dirk doubted it could get there ahead of him. "Do what you can."

"I will," the detective said. "Believe me."

As he clicked off, Dirk mulled over the discovery that Fred had killed his former girlfriend when they split up. It jibed with what police-science classes taught about spousal abusers.

He felt almost certain that Fred's intent was to claim Joni, not hurt her. The man wouldn't want to destroy the object of his obsession unless she rejected him.

But once she did, he would go after her with a vengeance.

FRED HELD AN UMBRELLA over Joni as they approached the front door. He had the bucket of chicken beneath the other arm.

She contemplated ditching the drinks and food sacks and making a run for it, but he was too close. The moment she tensed for action, he would notice.

Had everyone on the block already come home from work? Wasn't anyone giving a Halloween party? If only a car would turn onto the street, she could take the risk of running.

"You shouldn't have let Dirk stay with you," Fred said out of the blue. "That was wrong, Joni."

They reached the overhang. Setting the drinks on the porch, she fished out her key. "I didn't know who killed Lowell. I thought I needed protection."

"Did he touch you?" Fred closed the umbrella and set it aside. "Did you let him kiss you, Joni?"

Slimy, that was how this man made her feel. He ought to be crawling around in the garden with the rest of the slugs. Yet her life depended on placating him.

"Dirk's too much of a workaholic," she said. "I prefer a family man, like you."

Fred beamed. How could he be stupid enough to believe her? But he was hearing what he'd waited three years to hear.

"We belong together," he oozed. "Not here in this town. Too many gossips. We could go south. Mexico, maybe. Jeff would like that, don't you think?"

"Sure." She opened the door and went to the keypad. The code she'd chosen, a number she wasn't likely to forget but that didn't show up in her wallet, was Herb's birthday. Beneath Fred's gaze, she tapped in the date of Jeff's birthday.

Or was she mixed up? Maybe she'd intended to set Herb's birthday but instinctively used Jeff's. Suddenly Joni wasn't sure. She'd been so rattled about Kim's murder yesterday that she hadn't even set the alarm when she left for soccer practice, so she'd never had to de-activate it before. She could only hope now that she'd correctly punched in the wrong code.

Otherwise she'd be fleeing out the back with no alarm to summon help. Fred would have all the time in the world to hunt her down. He knew the woods better than she did. Obviously, he also felt comfortable scurrying around in the dark. But then, vermin usually did.

Behind her, he picked up the tray of drinks. Joni was about to cut through the den when it occurred to her that Dirk might have left some possessions in sight.

Instead, she went by the living room. Never mind that she was tracking mud onto the carpet. Nothing mattered except keeping a bright smile on her face while she dumped the food sacks onto the counter and moved to-ward the utility room.

"Where are you going?" Fred unloaded the drinks and the chicken.

"To get a sweater," she said as she went around the

corner. "And change my shoes." Kicking off the heels with a thump, she stepped into her canvas slip-ons.

Then she threw open the back door and ran as if the hounds of hell were after her.

THIS WAS A NIGHTMARE come to life, Dirk thought as traffic stopped ahead of him. He couldn't be more than a quarter of a mile from the turnoff and yet he was idling in place.

He shouldn't have accepted Charlie's guilt so readily. He should have insisted on staying with Joni. But blaming himself was useless. A tubby, middle-aged soccer dad had played them all for fools. So what was he going to do about it?

Gripping the wheel, Dirk studied the terrain.

The road had no shoulder, only a streaming gutter that separated it from a medium-high curb. There were no pedestrians in sight and, in this weather, little danger of encountering any.

He gauged the height of the curb and was grateful that, out of habit, he'd chosen a heavy rental car. It ought to be able to handle a steep tilt without flipping.

Time for a little offensive driving.

OPERATING ON INSTINCT, Joni turned left and scrambled toward Celia's house. Somewhere down the block, somebody had to be home.

Rain streamed down her face, making it hard to see more than a few feet ahead. Her slip-ons squelched and sucked in the mud, and her skirt clung to her thighs.

Where was Fred? She couldn't hear him and she didn't dare turn around to look.

Behind her, the alarm went off with a shocking blare. She stumbled, grabbed at a post and felt splinters rip her palm. It stung but she scarcely minded. She wasn't cold anymore, either. Nothing existed except this blind need to keep going.

A slope dropped before her, not long but very slick, and she lost her balance on the rim. Out of control, Joni plunged into Celia's backyard. She jolted down onto her hands, scraping her knees and twisting one leg. When she tried to straighten, pain shot through her calf.

"Joni!" It was Fred, some distance away. "Come back here!"

He was still in her yard. Maybe he hadn't seen her tumble.

She forced herself to stand, despite the stabbing in her leg. It was a muscle cramp, she told herself. She just needed to work it out.

If only Celia kept a key hidden somewhere…but there wasn't time to look. Fred would be searching this way any minute.

Unable to move at more than a hobble, Joni pressed close to the trees that divided the two properties. If she edged uphill, maybe she could circle around in the near-zero visibility and get back into her own house.

It wasn't much of a plan. Even with an injured leg, it would be difficult to climb the slope, cut across it and work her way down. She was as likely to run into Fred as to escape him.

Still it was a chance. Once indoors, she could lock him out. She could find a weapon.

The clanging bell formed a steady throb in her mind. Joni prayed that someone would hear it and that the police wouldn't disregard the alarm at their end.

She couldn't trust her life to luck. Despite the throbbing in her leg, she started upward.

DIRK BRACED AS HE TOOK the curb, half-expecting the air bag to inflate at the shock. It stayed mercifully in place.

The car's suspension and tires might never be the same again, he reflected as he eased forward at a pronounced tilt, but the steering didn't appear to be affected. Repressing an impulse to hit the gas, he drove at a slowly accelerating pace past the clot of cars.

Someone honked, but he ignored it. If the police noticed, so much the better.

Gravity did its best to pull him sideways, and water spewed from beneath the left tire. Holding his body rigid, Dirk concentrated on watching for obstacles ahead. Even so, he didn't see the cross street in time to brake. The car overshot the curb, crunched downward, caught its chassis on the raised concrete and then scraped free with a bone-rattling thud.

Dirk veered right. The rain hid the street sign, but this should be the entrance to Joni's development. He hoped he was right. If not, he might have just taken a fatal wrong turn.

Chapter Seventeen

Joni crouched among the trees, afraid to venture onto the low brush of the slope. Despite the darkness and heavy rain, she felt as if Fred would surely spot her.

Water dripped from her hair and clothing, and her fingers were going numb. The fall into Celia's yard had jolted her ribs and set them aching again. She hadn't, she realized, fully healed from her encounter with this maniac a week ago.

Only a week? It felt as if a lifetime had gone by.

Below her, a thump and a string of curses, barely audible over the alarm bell, revealed that he, too, had slid into Celia's yard. That meant her patio was clear. Unless, of course, he decided to turn back.

She had to make a run for it. Now.

Fighting a gust of wind, Joni staggered onto the open slope. She felt exposed, even though there was no reason to believe Fred could see her through the downpour any more than she could see him.

Losing her footing, she grabbed a bush, then felt sharp leaves cut her already lacerated palm. Tears sprang to her eyes, but she ignored them and kept angling downward. If only her feet didn't nearly pull loose from the slip-ons at every step. If only she had something to hold on to. If only she knew where Fred was.

Again she skidded, this time landing hard on her backside. Her skirt pulled up, and burrs stuck to her thighs. With rain sluicing down her face, she could barely make out the pale orb of light that marked the rear door below.

With a suddenness like a blow, the alarm cut off. Rain swished across the hillside, sounding abnormally loud.

For a terrified moment, Joni thought Fred had gone inside and deactivated the security system. Then she remembered that the bell shut off automatically after five minutes. She missed the jangling. It had aided in covering her movements, although it also helped Fred sneak around undetected.

Had he gone down through Celia's yard to the next house, hoping to pick up her trail, or was he heading back? Did he have a knife, maybe the one that had killed Kim DeLong?

Was it going to be Joni's blood on the patio this time?

In her mind, Fred no longer bore any resemblance to the benign father figure she'd sometimes wished Lowell would emulate. The fact that he'd been able to win people's trust and affection made him seem even more of a monster now.

A new sound made her heart leap. A car, coming up the street. She tensed, praying for the familiar growl of an engine tackling the steepness of her driveway.

It stopped too soon, before Celia's house. Too far away for the driver to hear her if she screamed, and that would alert Fred to her whereabouts.

Mentally, Joni calculated the rest of her descent. Between her and the patio, nearly invisible in the deluge, lay a stone retaining wall, then a four-foot drop to the rose bed. If she fell over it, Fred would hear the crash. Worse, she might be badly injured.

She had to take that risk. Keeping low to the ground, Joni sidled down the hill. Sooner than expected, her foot touched the hard, flat top of the retaining wall. At least she'd found it without falling over.

At this point, she remained virtually invisible although she knew her safety was illusory. She needed to make a run for it. Why wouldn't her muscles obey? Once she jumped down, Joni knew she would be silhouetted against the porch light. She felt stiff, cold and sore. And terrified.

Last Wednesday night, on this patio, horror had come out of nowhere. She could hardly believe, even now, that it had been Fred who attacked and not some virulent, unknowable force.

If she moved, it might find her again.

Inside the house lay warmth. Civilization. Jeff's childish world of toys and games. The bed where she and Dirk had made love.

She had to reach it. She had to try.

Into the void, Joni leaped.

WHILE VEERING FROM one street to another, operating largely on instinct, Dirk became aware of an alarm sounding a few blocks away. He wondered if it could be Joni's and who had set it off. He gave the car more gas, felt it start to hydroplane and forced himself to ease out of the skid.

The noise stopped abruptly. Why?

Dirk cursed aloud as he swung onto her street and saw how dark it was. But not at her house; someone had turned on the interior lights. Also the one on the patio.

Near the back edge of the house, a weak glow penetrated the pouring rain.

Could Fred be trying to re-create the scene of Lowell's murder?

Every fiber of his being shouted at Dirk to gun the motor and race to Joni's rescue. The impulse warred with his training, which demanded that he assess the situation and form a plan.

Well, he'd better do it in a damn hurry, he thought grimly. Because while he was sitting here deciding on a strategy, he might lose everything that mattered in this life.

JONI LANDED WITH A JOLT on the strip of grass between the rose bed and the concrete. The impact knocked her forward until the heels of her hands made raw contact with pavement. Her shoulders absorbed the blow with a wrenching throb. Her breath rasped, too loudly. For a moment, she couldn't move.

One of her shoes had flown off in the jump. No sense looking for it. She needed to get up, but the grass was slick. She staggered on all fours, regained her balance and straightened.

As she started moving, her head began to swim. It was like trying to run in a bad dream. She could see the back door but couldn't seem to reach it.

Then she noticed the silhouette near the garage. He'd come back. She could never reach the house before he did. But she had to do this, had to make it. For Jeff's sake. For Dirk's.

Joni flung herself forward.

As she stumbled across the hard surface, the cramp in her calf, nearly forgotten in the cold, shot white pain up through her leg. With a cry, she grabbed the glass table to keep from falling.

The man dived for her. She braced herself for the impact, but he didn't stop. As he went past, she made out the familiar beauty of broad shoulders and dark hair. Dirk!

She twisted, then saw why he'd bypassed her. Somehow Fred had gotten behind them. He must have circled around the front of the house to come at her from the opposite direction. Outfoxing her. Taking control.

He was shorter than Dirk but stockier, and he wielded a knife as smoothly as if it were an extension of himself. A superhuman madness glittered in his eyes.

She had to help. Maybe she could make it into the kitchen to fetch one of her own knives. No, the fire extinguisher would be better. Something with enough force to knock him over.

Joni took one step and her leg buckled. Her hands came down, ready to break her fall, but in midair the metal hose faucet caught her head with a mind-dimming whack.

DIRK HEARD JONI CRASH behind him. He knew she must be hurt, but he couldn't help her now.

He hadn't found so much as a jack in the rental car. Good sense had warned him to enter the house through the front and find a weapon, but he didn't want to take the time. Now only his martial-arts training could protect him against this madman.

Disarming a man with a blade wasn't usually difficult. Most people flailed wildly and struck from the outside, leaving their bodies vulnerable.

Not Allen Frederick Owens. Maybe he'd learned how

to fight in the marines. Dirk suspected his fanaticism helped even more.

The man's lips curled with fiendish glee as he performed a back-and-forth dance on the concrete. "You're a loser just like Lowell," he said. "Now you'll die like him."

"Lowell wasn't prepared for your attack." Dirk crouched, watching for an opening. *Let him lift his arms away from his body. Just for a second.* "It's easy killing helpless people, isn't it?"

Fred tossed the knife to his left hand, then back again, too quickly for Dirk to make his move. "You shouldn't be anywhere near Joni. You contaminate her, you piece of filth. But I'll make her clean again."

"Do you really think she could ever love you?" Dirk searched his opponent's face for a flicker of uncertainty, any sign that the man might be momentarily off guard. "We're lovers. Did she tell you that?"

"You're lying!" Rage bloated Fred's face, and he slashed fast and hard. The blade caught Dirk's jacket, inches from his stomach.

It hung there. In the split second before the knife was yanked free, Dirk lashed out with his foot, aiming to catch his opponent in the gut. But the man dodged away, reclaiming the knife as he went. With a roar, he lunged and slashed at Dirk's thigh, slicing the pants and drawing a stripe of blood.

Pain clawed up his leg. Dirk ignored it and resumed his fighting stance.

The two men faced each other, breathing hard. Fred bared his teeth and snarled like a wild animal. An animal possessed of feral cunning. And the scent of blood could only make it more dangerous.

JONI FOUGHT THE DARKNESS. Something was wrong. Lowell. Someone had attacked Lowell.

Her head hurt. She remembered someone grabbing her and slamming her skull against the hummingbird feeder. She recalled, just a moment ago, the sticky sugar water pouring over her neck and cheeks.

The men were still there, facing off on the patio. She saw the knife in Fred's hand, just as it had been before. But the man with his back to her wasn't Lowell. She knew the compactness of his frame, the grace with which he moved. It was Dirk.

Lowell and Fred—that had been last week. The memory of that event must have lain buried in some deep recess of her mind. Now it was happening all over again. If she didn't find a way to stop it, this time it would be Dirk lying dead on the patio.

DIRK UNDERSTOOD that he had made the nearly fatal error of underestimating his opponent. He wouldn't do it again.

He shifted to keep Joni's crumpled form behind him. Fred would have to kill him to reach her.

On the hill, the downpour intensified, although a moment ago he wouldn't have thought that possible. Even here beneath the patio cover, rain was hitting sideways against Dirk's overheated skin.

The business suit cramped his movements. He wished he had Fred's ease of action in a sweatshirt and jeans. But Dirk had once disabled an armed robber even though his own gun jammed. He had also, in a burst of adrenaline, foiled a kidnap attempt by shoving an overweight businessman up half a dozen steps and through a doorway.

He wasn't going to let a minor annoyance like a suit

jacket get in his way. Not when there was so much at stake.

At least this time he knew the other man's weakness. Jealousy. He must use it to goad Fred.

"You can't have her," Dirk panted. "She doesn't want you and she never will. Haven't you figured that out yet?"

The blade quivered. Dirk tensed, ready.

He was so focused on the knife that he almost didn't notice Fred's subtle change of position. As Dirk tried to jump away, a foot shot out and caught him on the side of the leg. If it had hit his knee, as intended, he would've been disabled. Instead, it knocked him off balance just enough to give Fred an opening.

The man darted in for the final thrust. A blast of water hit him directly in the face. Dirk dived and rolled under the stinging spray, toward his sputtering foe. Toward the knife Fred had just dropped.

Their hands met on the haft. The water stopped. Joni, hose in hand, couldn't hit one without hitting the other.

This was hand-to-hand fighting, no-holds-barred. Dirk knew all the dirty tricks. He knew where to kick and where to gouge. But Fred's sheer raging madness gave him an edge. It made him close his fingers over the blade itself, forcing Dirk's hand away. It enabled him to smash his forehead into Dirk's and keep going through the shock.

Toward Joni.

SHE SAW DIRK GO DOWN. She didn't know how badly he was hurt. Maybe another blast of water would protect him, but between the disorienting shadows and the thrumming in her head, she could scarcely tell one looming shape from the other.

By the time she saw Fred swooping toward her, he was too close. She couldn't swing the nozzle into position.

A booming sound filled her head, as if a great wind had hit the patio. Fred stopped, surprise rendering his evil face suddenly childlike.

Earthquake? she wondered dazedly. But earthquakes didn't strike precisely when you needed them. They also didn't make a man clutch the front of his sweatshirt and crumple to the ground.

Footsteps scuffed behind Joni. "You can put the hose down now, Mrs. Peterson." Someone reached around and removed the nozzle.

"It's about time you got here." Dirk sat up, rubbing his head. "I don't suppose you put in a good word with the paramedics?"

"They're on their way," Detective MacDougall said, and caught Joni as her knees gave out.

"KATHRYN'S TAKING the boys to Herb's place," Dirk reported a short time later as they waited in the kitchen. Another detective was on his way to question them, since MacDougall had been involved in the shooting. "Then she'll go to the police station to tell them what she knows."

"She's a good person," Joni said. "What happened is not her fault."

"I hope she understands that. She'll have enough to deal with now." Dirk stopped. "We're not supposed to discuss the case."

"I know." MacDougall had allowed them to wait together only after they promised not to talk about what had happened. He wanted to make sure their testimony wasn't compromised.

Not that it would make any difference. This time, Joni had no fear of forgetting.

Once she grasped that Fred Owens was dead, relief had cleared her mind. She had even remembered to ask that a patrolman break the news gently to his mother. She hoped that Edith's closeness to Kathryn and Bobby would help her weather this blow.

Although the paramedics had offered to transport Dirk and Joni to the hospital, they had both declined. She had, however, allowed the men to bandage her right hand, and they'd checked but found no sign of concussion.

The crime-scene investigators had discovered suspicious hairs and bloodstains in the back of Fred's van. That, coupled with other evidence and Joni's restored memory of last Wednesday, was likely to close the books on Lowell's and Kim's deaths. There was no further reason for Dirk to hang around Viento del Mar.

Joni didn't want to come home from the hospital in a day or so and find him gone. She intended to stick around for what little time he remained in town.

"I'm going to sell the house," she said abruptly. "We can't stay here after this."

Dirk's eyes met hers across the table. A bruise purpled his forehead, and she knew his leg must be hurting, but warmth suffused his face. "It does have a few wonderful memories, though."

She glanced down at her scraped hands. "Also little pieces of me scattered all over it."

"Oh, by the way..." Dirk reached inside his jacket. "Happy birthday."

She didn't want to hear about birthdays, not another reminder after all Fred's prattling. But when she saw the velvet jeweler's box, she knew Dirk must have gone to a lot of trouble. He'd bought something for her to remember him by. As if she needed anything. As if his scent and his voice and his way of glancing at her sideways weren't seared into her heart.

"That was...very thoughtful." She let the case rest on her palm. What was inside hardly mattered because the only gift she wanted was sitting across from her, a smile teasing the corners of his mouth.

"Well?" he said. "Aren't you going to open it?"

Through the window, she could hear police officers calling to each other. It was beginning to be a familiar sound. Way too familiar.

"Sure." Joni pried at the tight lid. It took a couple of attempts to get the box open.

It was empty. Inside she saw nothing but a pink satin lining bearing the name of the town jewelry store.

"Is it supposed to be this way?" she asked.

Dirk chuckled. "I wasn't robbed, if that's what you mean."

"Well, it's lovely," Joni joked. "A girl can always use a few of these."

His hands closed over hers, enfolding them in warmth. "It's empty," he said, "because I didn't know what kind of wedding ring you wanted."

She couldn't believe she'd heard correctly. Maybe she wanted to hear the words so badly that she'd misinterpreted him.

"I'm not sure I understand," she said.

"I'm asking you to marry me." He leaned across the table until his head nearly touched hers. "Battered and bruised as I am, I promise I'll clean up and make a respectable husband."

It wasn't easy to resist the urge to shout, "Yes!" But Joni knew that happy endings only grew from sturdy roots.

"Your work is overseas," she said. "Isn't it?"

He sat back but didn't let go of her hands. "The answer's been growing on me all week. I've got a lot of companies already established and, with some adjustments, I can manage them from here most of the time."

"But don't you love a challenge? Starting something new?" she asked.

"I am starting something new, or at least launching something Lowell started," he said. "The publishing business. The more I get involved, the more I'm enjoying it. I suspect it will keep me occupied for a long time to come."

Joni had to get everything out in the open. There couldn't be any doubts, for either of them. "I thought you didn't want to be tied down."

"Commitment felt like a ball and chain," he conceded. "I guess it took coming back to Viento del Mar, being around you and Jeff, to realize I was allowing myself to be haunted by my own childhood. I was afraid to relinquish control, to let myself be vulnerable."

"Now you're not?" she demanded.

"It happened anyway." Dirk gave her a rueful grin. "The two of you sneaked into my heart. Joni, you're not just the woman I love. You're my soul mate. You're part of me. Getting married is only a formality."

Laughter bubbled inside her. She didn't want this moment to end. She wanted to stretch it out and savor every nuance.

"So when did you change your mind?" she asked. "You didn't even give me a hint this morning."

He glanced down at the jeweler's box. "When I picked this up, my intention was to let you select whatever jewelry you wanted. But even then I think I was picturing a ring in here."

"So this is kind of a spur-of-the-moment thing?" she persisted.

His eyes flashed blue fire. "I've always known there was a piece missing inside me, but I didn't think it could be found. Tonight, when I nearly lost you, I realized that without you, my world isn't merely incomplete. It doesn't exist. I know I deserve to be tortured, but please put me out of my misery. Marry me, Joni."

She ran her thumb along his cheek and gazed into his bruised, fierce, loving face. "Try to stop me," she said.

Chapter Eighteen

If a blizzard hadn't hit Moscow, Dirk would have made it home in time for his first anniversary. As it was, it took two extra days to catch a plane out of Russia.

Then, if his connecting flight in London hadn't been canceled due to fog, at least he would have made it home before Thanksgiving. Instead, he got stuck for an extra day, spent nearly twenty hours in transit and arrived bleary-eyed in Los Angeles on the holiday with a two-hour drive ahead of him.

It was, he supposed, what he deserved for spending three weeks away from home. Travel held less and less appeal these days, except for the few times when Joni was able to travel with him.

As the publishing business got under way, she'd given up her public relations job and taken to editing with boundless excitement. Where Dirk enjoyed hunting down cutting-edge subject matter and authors, his wife had the patience for details and an instinct for identifying what wasn't working on the page.

They made a good team, he reflected as he drove north on the freeway toward Viento del Mar. After three weeks away from her, he didn't dare dwell on all the ways in which they fitted together or he might steer right off the road.

At least he'd be home in time for Thanksgiving dinner at their new house in a pleasant development north of downtown. By now, cooking aromas must be drifting from kitchen to den to cathedral-ceilinged living room, all the way upstairs to Jeff's room.

Selling the old Peterson estate hadn't been difficult once Mrs. Wright decided to accept a generous pension and move near her sister in Florida. Joni's old house had presented more difficulty because it had been the scene of a murder. Finally, Celia Lu had bought it as a rental. That way, she'd told them, she could always be sure of having neighbors whose company she enjoyed.

The investigation of Lowell's and Kim's murders had been formally closed. With the perpetrator dead, no further action was necessary.

Joni had dropped assault charges against Charlie Rogers after he agreed that he needed more counseling. He was no longer coaching soccer, but he still taught adult fitness and had had no further problems.

Although Edith Owens might never fully recover from her son's death, she'd admitted to the police that she knew he was capable of violence and had sometimes feared him herself. Moving in with Kathryn and Bobby gave her renewed purpose in life and helped all of them recover.

Both Herb and Jeff had been happy to learn the truth about Jeff's parentage. In fact, Herb had confided, he'd been intending to tell Joni not to let that fool Dirk get away because he would make a terrific father.

He was a father all right, Dirk reflected, warming at the memory of reading bedtime stories to Jeff. And accompanying him to ball games. And helping with his new hobby of building models of spaceships.

He wished he'd been part of Jeff's life earlier. Not that he would've wanted to deprive Lowell of the experience, but watching Joni as the baby grew inside her, witnessing the birth and seeing those first baby steps would've been a miracle beyond imagining.

Well, his cup was already overflowing. It was pure indulgence to wish for anything more.

Clouds hovered all the way to Santa Barbara and then the sun broke through. Dirk gave a sigh of satisfaction. He'd had enough bad weather on this trip to last him a long time.

Downtown Viento del Mar was shuttered except for the supermarket at the corner of San Bernardo Road. Dirk had called ahead and offered to pick up any items Joni needed, but she'd said that all she wanted was the sight of him, and the sooner the better.

He pushed back a hank of hair, askew from having been slept on crookedly aboard the plane. He should have gotten a cut last week but preferred to wait for his regular barber.

For a moment, when his hand brushed his forehead, Dirk flashed back to that Halloween night when he'd nearly lost Joni. The scars had faded in a year, but the trauma recurred now and again.

He could still see Fred's lunging shape and feel the slash of the knife on his leg. Could still hear Joni behind him, crashing against the faucet.

With time, though, the shock had softened. Now he could accept that night as a kind of crucible in which his old life had been melted down and transformed into a far better one.

A mile past downtown, Dirk turned left into the new

development. The yards were small but brightened, even
at this time of year, by well-tended flower beds. In front
of several houses, people were getting out of cars, carrying covered dishes.

A surge of gratitude welled inside him that he was
part of a family, too. That he was only a few blocks
away from the sure and steady center of his universe.

He approached slowly, drinking in the sight of the
two-story house with its windows aglow. In front, rosebushes burst forth with a final bloom, the scarlets and
pinks so vivid that they stood out even in the twilight.

From the absence of a sports car parked in front, Dirk
could see that his grandfather hadn't arrived yet. According to Joni, Herb would be bringing his new girlfriend, a lively widow.

At the touch of his finger on the remote control, the
garage door slid open. Dirk pulled in next to Joni's car.

The interior door flew open and Jeff's head poked out.
"Dad?" he called. Then, over his shoulder, "Dad's
home! Can I tell him yet?"

Tell him what?

As he got out, delicious cooking smells flooded
around Dirk, even better than he'd fantasized. He could
detect turkey and stuffing and pumpkin pie.

Jeff came running out. There wasn't room to swing
him around; besides, the boy was getting too big for such
antics. But Dirk picked him up in a bear hug, all the
same.

"Can I carry your suitcase?" his son asked as he was
set down.

"It's a bit heavy, but you can handle my carry-on."
Dirk lifted luggage from the trunk. "That's got the good
stuff in it anyway."

"Good stuff?"

"Oh, presents. But you wouldn't be interested in anything like that."

The boy shot him a knowing look and reached for the bag. He marched proudly ahead of Dirk into the house.

Joni came from the kitchen to greet them. Her blond hair, cut in a chin-length pageboy, haloed her head as she wiped her hands on her apron.

It was such a domestic gesture that Dirk almost couldn't believe this same woman would, in a few days, rip through the new manuscripts he'd acquired and critique them within an inch of their lives.

He dropped his suitcase barely in time to catch her as she flew into his arms. She felt hot and alive against his cool body, which didn't stay cool for long.

He wished the cooking and the imminent arrival of guests and even their son's excitement could be suspended while he carried Joni upstairs. Three weeks ago, they'd said farewell after a lovemaking session that lasted most of the night. This time, he figured they'd need the entire four-day weekend.

"You feel wonderful," Joni murmured into his ear.

"He brought presents!" Jeff called. "Can I open the bag, Daddy?"

To his wife, Dirk whispered, "If you think I feel good now, just wait till later." To his son, he said, "If you're careful. There's a package with your name on it."

Reluctantly releasing Joni, he shrugged out of his overcoat and carried his large suitcase upstairs so it would be out of the way. Heading back down, he nearly collided with Jeff, who had opened his package to discover an intricate plastic model of a Russian spaceship, ready to be assembled. "I've never seen this one before! I can't wait to get started."

"It won't be on the market for another month. Need any help with that?"

Dirk was relieved when he received a resounding "No! I can handle it." Much as he enjoyed building models with his son, he had other priorities right now.

When he reached the kitchen, Joni was removing a pan of stuffing from the oven. "You look terrific, considering what you've been through the past few days. Airport lounges aren't exactly my idea of luxurious lodgings."

Dirk regarded her longingly. "I'm not going away again for a long, long time." Then he remembered his son's words earlier. "What was it Jeff wanted to tell me?"

Joni removed the apron. Underneath, she wore a fuzzy pink sweater and tan slacks. "Are you planning to go anywhere next July?"

"I don't think so," he said. "Why? Is there some kind of publishing conference?"

"If there is, you'll have to cancel." Mischief danced in her eyes.

"Why?" He knew she was up to something, but all he could think about was kissing her until they both got dizzy.

"Well, I assume you'll want to be in the delivery room," she said.

He stared at her, hardly daring to grasp the implication. "We're—you're—pregnant?"

"I took a home test two days ago." She beamed at him. "I didn't mean to tell Jeff, but he saw the kit in the bathroom and asked me what it meant."

"It's all right." Gently, he gathered his wife against him. "Maybe you should sit down. Are you sure that belt isn't too tight? Could it be cutting off the oxygen supply or something?"

She laughed. "I'm not made out of porcelain. And I've had a baby before, remember?"

He had dozens of questions, most of which she probably couldn't answer yet. Whether it was a boy or a girl. What name they should choose. How soon they'd be able to see it on an ultrasound.

"I can't believe it," he admitted. "I was going to ask how you'd feel about having another child, but I wanted to give us all time to settle in."

"I'd say we're pretty settled." She stroked the hair back from his forehead. "You'll recall we forgot to take precautions before you left. Maybe that wasn't entirely a mistake."

"Maybe it wasn't a mistake at all," he conceded. "I figured you knew what you were doing. I certainly did."

"Now we've made a baby two different ways," she teased. "The results may be the same, but this method was more fun."

He wanted to say more, but the doorbell rang. "Would that be Herb?"

"And Mary Anne. She's quite a character. You'll like her." Joni winked. "Maybe by next Thanksgiving, we'll have a new member of the family." With a glance at her stomach, she amended, "Make that two new members."

"You're matchmaking!"

"Herb didn't need my help." She started for the door. "He found this lady himself."

Dirk lingered behind, treasuring the miraculous news she'd given him. It was impossible to absorb the implications all at once, but, he decided, he didn't need to. Half the fun of life was being surprised along the way.

With a prayer of thanksgiving humming through his mind, he straightened his tie and went to help his wife greet their guests.

Amnesia...
an unknown danger...
a burning desire.
With

HARLEQUIN®

I N T R I G U E®

you're just

A MEMORY AWAY

from passion, danger...
and love!

Look for all the books in this exciting new miniseries:

Missing: One temporary wife
#507 THE MAN SHE MARRIED
by Dani Sinclair in March 1999

Mission: Find a lost identity
#511 LOVER, STRANGER
by Amanda Stevens in April 1999

Seeking: An amnesiac's daughter
#515 A WOMAN OF MYSTERY
by Charlotte Douglas in May 1999

A MEMORY AWAY—where remembering the truth becomes a matter of life, death...and love!

Available wherever Harlequin books are sold.

HARLEQUIN®
Makes any time special ™

Look us up on-line at: http://www.romance.net   HIAMA

MURDER AT THE MOVIES

CHARLENE WEIR
GEORGE BAXT
MAXINE O'CALLAGHAN

MURDER TAKE TWO
by Charlene Weir

Hollywood comes to Hampstead, Kansas, with the filming of a
new picture starring sexy actress Laura Edwards. But murder
steals the scene when a stunt double is impaled on a pitchfork.

THE HUMPHREY BOGART MURDER CASE
by George Baxt

Hollywood in its heyday is brought to life in this witty caper
featuring a surprise sleuth—Humphrey Bogart. While filming
The Maltese Falcon, he searches for a real-life treasure, dodging
a killer on a murder trail through Hollywood.

SOMEWHERE SOUTH OF MELROSE
by Maxine O'Callaghan

P.I. Delilah West is hired to search for an old high school
classmate. The path takes her through the underbelly of broken
dreams and into the caprices of fate, where secrets are born and
sometimes kept....

Available March 1999 at your favorite retail outlet.

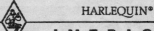

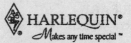